LONDON LIES

URBAN TALES FROM LIARS' LEAGUE

EDITED BY
CHERRY POTTS AND KATY DARBY

ARACHNE PRESS

This collection first published in UK 2012 by Arachne Press
100 Grierson Road, London SE23 1NX
www.arachnepress.com
London Lies © 2012 Arachne Press
ISBN: 978-1-909208-00-1
 Edited by Cherry Potts and Katy Darby
The moral rights of the authors have been asserted
All content is copyright the respective authors.
For copyright on individual stories see page 3
All stories originally performed at Liars' League and published
on their website 2007-2012
The Runner Alan McCormick previously published in *Dogsbodies
and Scumsters*, by Alan McCormick, Roast Books 2011

Printed and bound by TJ International Ltd, Padstow, Cornwall

Martin Pengelly would like to acknowledge the sources for his titles: *Incurable Romantic Seeks Dirty Filthy Whore* is a painting by Harland Miller; *Girl with Palmettes* is a painting by Malcolm Drummond.

Contents

The Suitcase
Rosalind Stopps

It is everybody's duty to be on the alert for terrorists and snipers in London these days, but as a senior assistant in a shoe shop in a large precinct, I am obviously used to living on the front line. Things are not necessarily what they seem, that's the important thing to remember. You have to look behind the obvious for the extra something that might be lurking there, rather like when you meet someone's boyfriend or husband.

'This is Kevin,' they might say, as if they are letting you in on one of life's great secrets. You look up, expecting to see a handsome man or a kindly man, or better still, a mixture of the two, like David Attenborough, but instead, Kevin is standing there in an ill-fitting coat, looking like a man who sells lawn mowers in December. This hasn't happened to me often, but one thing you may notice about me is that I have a great imagination. I am a woman who knows that when the scary side of life comes along, it will lurk behind something else, something with a smile and a bag of sweets to offer to small children.

I am good at anticipating lone gunmen. I can put myself right inside their heads, and imagine what could make them behave like that. They might have lost their job, for example, through no fault of their own. Someone might have spiked their drink at the office party, and taken photos of them with their trousers round their ankles, or spread vicious rumours about them, saying that they were too fat to have children, or had a gun at home when they didn't, and that could have made them mad or sad enough to go and get one.

I felt like that at school, when everyone thought that I had stolen Carol Eliot's rubber. It was shaped like a tortoise, and I admired it, I never denied that. I didn't steal it though, I swear I didn't, but I did steal some other people's rubbers after that, just to show them what it was like. I cut most of them into pieces with a razor blade so I know a bit about regret, as well. I think I would make a good mother, full of insights and wisdom.

When I got on the underground train that morning at the Elephant and Castle, it was obviously me who noticed it first. Maureen was one step behind me, dithering with her Oyster card and calculating her fertile period, and she didn't even notice anything unusual.

'Unusual?' I said, 'That is a rather mild way of putting it.' I can be a bit sarcastic, and I know that it is not the most polite thing to be, but a large unattended suitcase by the door of an underground train is a lot more than unusual.

'It's probably someone who forgot, and got off without it,' Maureen said, which has to rank as one of the most stupid things I have ever heard her say. And believe me, there have been a few. Recently, she told me that the reason she and Kevin haven't been able to get pregnant yet is because their bedroom faces south, and that can have a bad effect on the whole life force thing. Last month, it was because a pigeon had landed on her windowsill two mornings in a row.

'Why would anyone leave a suitcase of that size?' I asked. I have always been logical as well as imaginative, and I don't take anything at face value. I'm not the kind of person who would allow a complete stranger to use the shop's toilet, for example, even if they appeared to be in quite urgent need.

What I was thinking, which had obviously not struck Maureen, was that a lone crazed gunman could have left his gun in the case all ready to go on a killing spree, and sat in another carriage. I have always believed that a bit of preparation is necessary for most things – warming the teapot before putting the bags in, wearing loose boxers to let the sperm breathe, or buying a jacket with enough pockets to store the ammunition for a mass murder.

I looked at the suitcase more closely, not going too near just in case it was a bomb that had changed hands for vast amounts of money in the criminal world. Or a landmine, that someone might want to plant in a garden for revenge or even spite; there is no accounting for the lengths some people will go to. Last week I read a story in the newspaper about a man who threw acid on a small dog because his ex-wife had got to keep it. The dog had to be put down.

I stood back near the door as the train hurtled through the tunnel to Borough station, and leaned as far forward with my upper body as I could without falling. It looked like an ordinary suitcase. It had a dial at the top, the kind where you click it round to the right numbers and the case opens.

'We'll have to stop the train and call the police,' I said, 'they were very specific about that on the anti-terrorism leaflet that came to all the shops last year.'

Maureen didn't look happy.

'Don't worry,' I said and it was nice to be able to say something so helpful. 'I'll deal with it. I watched a programme about the bomb squad, and I think that the main thing is not to jolt it.'

Maureen looked so relieved that I stood up a bit taller. This must be what heads of families feel like, I thought, men and women with children, who bring home the food, fix the taps and unblock the drains. It must be like being on the first float in a bank holiday parade, with everyone clapping and shouting and babies waving small flags.

The carriage was empty apart from us, and I thought how lucky it was that Maureen and I are always so early. We have been the first retail assistants to arrive on the premises for 52 days out of the last 70, and we keep it written down in a little book in the staff room, in case anyone says that we are late. I suppose that will all change if Maureen does get pregnant.

I had some little socks in my pocket, the kind we use if someone comes in to the shop to try on shoes with bare feet. It's obviously not appropriate, putting sweaty feet into brand new shoes that somebody else might end up spending quite a lot of money on, but you would be surprised at how many people try to do it, even people with noticeably poor foot hygiene. I thought about fingerprints and ignored the slight smell. Of course, they didn't have fingers so it was like wearing mittens, but I really didn't have much choice. I circled the suitcase to see where I could get the best grip, while Maureen hovered in the aisle stepping from foot to foot in her silver shoes as if it was a new dance that she had invented.

'Go to the back of the carriage,' I said, 'in case anything goes wrong.' I liked the feeling of being in charge for once. We're supposed to be more or less equal in the shop, both paid the same, but she tends to boss me about a bit. I think it's because she is married. I've noticed that about married people, there's a kind of smugness about having a special person who thinks you are great that carries over into areas of your life where really, you are no better than anyone else. Maybe it is the promise of regular sex.

I decided not to touch the handle on the grounds that if I was going to booby trap a suitcase, I would make very sure that the handle was the trigger. Most people wouldn't think of this, but I am not most people, so I kind of encircled the case in my arms like a sleepy child, and picked it up. It wasn't heavy, and that was a surprise.

It was very important not to jolt the case at all. I stood up really gradually, moving my hands just a tiny bit to get a better grip, and cursing the slipperiness of the socks covering my fingers. The case felt as if it was empty except for one thing, and whatever that was shifted about a bit if I wasn't very careful. No-one looked at me as I left the tunnel, Maureen following at a safe distance like a private detective on the trail of a cheating spouse. I balanced on the escalator and walked on tiptoes through London Bridge Station, locked in a sweaty embrace with the suitcase.

The bag seemed to shake a little by the pasty stand, or it might have been my hands slipping, and I almost dropped it in surprise. I felt proud that I managed not to. I thought that there might be a busload of pensioners just outside, or a party of tiny children in wheelchairs, and if the case was loaded with explosives they could be hurt. The only hope was to hang on, do one good thing regardless of my personal safety and hope that someone somewhere noticed. Maybe the man who worked in the shoe-mending kiosk would finally notice me, and although I would be sad to have been blown to pieces, the thought of him and others crying at the tragedy made it all seem a little more worthwhile. Who knows, maybe there would be a picture of me over the front of the station when they rebuilt it, or a small plaque in my memory. People would call their children 'Barbara' in the hope that they would one day be as daring, and as brave, and Maureen might see me in a different light.

I wanted to take the bag to the river, but I wasn't at all sure which direction it was in. I am not the kind of person who asks for directions, even in an extreme situation, so we danced out of the front, the suitcase and I, past the black cabs and looking for signs of water. Not a sail or a mast in sight, and wherever the bridge had gone to it certainly wasn't here. I am resourceful though, and I spotted a large skip, taller than me and over by the building works in the corner. There was a big chute going in to it like a children's slide in an adventure playground, still quiet as if the children were all in bed. If I could hurl the case in and drop down flat to the pavement, I might still have a chance even if there was a bomb inside.

I whispered a quick goodbye to the case at the skip and raised it up above my head in slow motion, ready to throw and taking care not to jolt it any more than I could help. The noise of a city getting ready to face the day seemed to stop for a moment, and I wondered if this was the last time I would feel the pavement beneath my feet, or look up at the sun climbing over the docklands skyscrapers.

It was easier to throw than I thought, and I aimed well. There was a soft thud as it hit the bottom, and I wanted to drop to the floor but I settled for bending as if to do up my shoelaces instead, in case anyone was watching. I needn't have worried. There was no flash, no explosion lighting the air like a memory of the Blitz. Just that soft thud and a tiny sound that could have been a cat, or a squeaky toy, and then all the cars seemed to start again, and I could hear an ambulance on its way to the hospital.

*

It was the ambulance that made me think of it. The ambulance going past, and the way that the suitcase in my arms had felt like someone I hadn't met yet.

What if there'd been a baby in there, I thought, a real baby that somebody didn't want? I wished that I hadn't thrown it so hard or so far. The skip was too tall for me to climb in, and the station forecourt was starting to fill up like the opening scene in a play. If only I had been brave enough to open the case. I would have been so happy to see a baby, blinking in the light as if she had just come out of the cinema on a sunny afternoon. I could picture Maureen's face, looking at me as if I was the best work colleague a woman could have.

We could have kept it in the shop, me and Maureen, made a little cradle from a shoebox and taken turns to feed it. The customers would have loved it, and I might have even been promoted to manager when central office heard how business had picked up.

I turned to give Maureen a thumbs up and heard a rumble as the first rubble of the day flew down the chute and covered the suitcase, until it was nothing more than a memory of what might have been.

Maureen and I went back into the station. We could still be at the shop before it opened if we caught the next train, and I have always thought that punctuality is vital in the shoe industry.

Thieves We Were
Simon Hodgson

In the spring that my father died, we walked through the confetti of Japanese cherry blossom in the Elsted churchyard after the ten o'clock service and he told me for the first time about the Reverend Norton Mudge.

Although my father didn't talk about his childhood, I knew he'd grown up in the East End, that rabbit warren of brick-built houses thrown up after the Second World War. Patrick Delaney had been born in Bethnal Green, half a mile from York Hall, the fabled home of British boxing. One September night he'd taken me up to London on the train, to a smoky gymnasium where we'd sat three deep in the narrow gallery and watched lean white men, as pale and nervous as whippets, fight three rounds apiece.

It was smaller than I'd expected, and darker, a cavern smelling of Pall Mall cigarettes and sweat and the Vaseline smeared on the faces of the fighters. At the beginning and end of each bout, the announcer would clamber into the ring, a fat man in black trousers ducking awkwardly between the ropes as the crowd fell silent, and for a moment it felt like a church.

Reverend Mudge, Patrick said, appeared in Bethnal Green during the war and having earned his right to preach beneath the bomb bays of the Luftwaffe, he remained there for the next fifteen years. A Suffolk man, he found a home among the hotchpotch of Cockneys, Irish and Jews who attended his services. Anyone was welcome at St Mary's, he joked, if only for the tea and biscuits afterwards.

Out of these quiet neighbourly mornings came the open house afternoons, in which parishioners laid on cakes and home-made lemonade in their front rooms. Mudge knew the value of his community and reached out to its most distant members: the broken; the begging; the walking wounded who wore medals on their overcoats even in summer; the unemployed; the needy; the mentally ill, whose smiles and sudden rages passed like clouds across the sun; the infirm; the elderly; even those to whom confession meant thirty feet of chain round the ankles and a five-fathom dip in the Thames.

Pinchbeck Wilson was his name. Pinch, they called him. The lord of the manor, the greatest gangster on the Hackney Road and the only man from whom my father ever stole. Wilson and Mudge were from opposite sides of the fence, in terms of the Good Book, but Pinch had heard about the clergyman's service in the Blitz, carrying water, clearing rubble, conducting services in the gloom of Aldgate East tube station, four floors underground, as the lights flickered and flinched at the metal rain above.

Wilson himself had fought with some distinction in France and the Low Countries, although he lost any chance of medals after he was caught pilfering the regiment's collection of captured German sidearms. According to dad's friend Danny Harris, Pinch kept an entrenching tool from his time in France, with an edge whetted so sharp a man could see his own face in it before he died. Wilson once used the blade to sever an associate's wrist tendons, then later to dig his grave in the marshes west of Purfleet. Nothing good ever came out of them marshes, Pinch used to say, but plenty of bad went in.

Stories of Pinch Wilson were legion in that part of London, my dad said, adding that most of them were probably myths. Other boys' fathers told them tales of riches and robberies, of Wilson's murderous associates. Of the hauls he'd made in the years following the war, when the police were more interested in public unrest than his quiet lorryloads of stolen goods. Of the strange old woman, some said Russian, or Hungarian, who hid him when the cops came looking.

Patrick's dad told him no such tales. Hugh Delaney had confidence in his boy, sure that the lad would learn in his own time the difference between truth and lies. He was also tired. By the time my father was nine, Hugh was already a widower of 51, only a greying whisker short of Norton Mudge's age. He'd survived the war, survived the army and made it home only for his bride to die three years later of an infection caused by inhaling the concrete dust and smoke from the charred urban rubble. He was not a talkative father, but he did give his son one piece of advice.

'Never take anything he offers you.'

Even aged nine, Patrick knew what that meant. Pinch Wilson was a generous man, but somehow, all his gifts came back to him. Eddie O'Neill, the bookie on Mare Street, at the very edge of Pinch's territory, had over-extended himself a few years back. Pinch offered him a loan, 'to get yourself back on your feet'. He now owned the book-makers, while Eddie drank for a living at The Green Man on Cambridge Heath Road.

Or Albert Isen, the publican: he ran The Earl Grey, until Pinch went halves with him. Inside six months, Albert found out that his share was nearer a quarter and some Fridays, not even that. After his teenage son was braced one night under the railway bridge, he sold his share in the pub and moved east to Essex. Pinchbeck Wilson threw him a leaving bash to remember and pulled pints of Fuller's London Pride 'til two in the morning.

He drove a Jaguar Mark II the colour of day-old blood and when he parked on the road, kids from three streets away would cluster around and listen with open eyes to the engine ticking as it warmed down. Scallies, he called them, scallywags, a remnant of Glaswegian slang from a stint in the Bar-L. Wilson had been nicked up in Scotland, claimed Brendan, while taking car parts off a ship in the Clyde. Brendan's father was from

Falkirk and knew about these things.

That profitable northern enterprise nearly earned Wilson four thousand pounds for nine hours work, but instead cost him two and a half years as a guest of Her Majesty in Barlinnie, the toughest prison in Scotland. The time wasn't wasted. Pinch made contacts inside, contacts he sent for when he got back to London. Which is how Murdo McLean, who'd done two years for assault, two for extortion and four for armed robbery, happened to be passing out custard creams at Reverend Mudge's parish party.

Once a year, Pinch Wilson would open his doors to Bethnal Green. Not all the doors, my father added. Guests were allowed in the back garden, the front room and the kitchen – Mudge called it 'the parlour' when he informed the children who'd turned up mob-handed. Most of the two-storey houses in Hackney Borough had a passageway so you could walk from the street to the garden, but Pinch's house had a heavy wooden door with a lock and no spaces between the slats for peeking. This from Danny Harris, who'd tried exactly that.

The garden was a balding square of grass with a six-foot brick wall at the end that backed onto the knobbled alleyway where the lock-ups and garages were. Two or three kids were kicking a stone between them, watched carefully by Murdo, when my father went into the kitchen.

'Can I help ya, son?' Murdo materialised from behind him, blocking out the light from the garden. He wasn't a tall man, perhaps only five foot nine, but he was wide. Broad in the chest, thick in the neck and the wrist and the ankle. McLean was muscle, used mostly by Wilson for show, occasionally for heavier work. He was built, my father said with an apologetic wrinkle of his eyebrow, like a brick shithouse. He told Murdo he was looking for the toilet.

'Doon the hall fust door on the right.' But Patrick Delaney didn't go right. He opened the door on the left to Pinch

Wilson's study, opening it just enough to slip through and into a room darkened by the closed curtains. Before him was a desk with envelopes and a black fountain pen, three drawers on the right side.

By the door, a small cabinet with shelves: files on the bottom, a clawhammer beside a green Lyle's Golden Syrup tin filled with nails, a few paperbacks, two rings of keys and a pair of calfskin gloves in fine brown leather. On the top shelf was a tin of Tom Long 'grand old rich tobacco', a silver hip flask, four tickets to a show at the Royal Court theatre on Sloane Square, and Pinchbeck Wilson's entrenching tool.

It was heavier than Patrick expected, spade-shaped, but smaller, with a worn wooden handle as long as a pencil and a silver blade that tapered to a sharp edge. On the back were words he recognised as German, but he didn't know what they said. He held it in both hands, feeling its heft, then lifted it up to his face. There was no reflection, or was that just the darkness? He put it back on the shelf and slipped the hip flask into his pocket.

Patrick rejoined the little crew in the garden and opened his palms to show the Garibaldi biscuits he'd swiped from the kitchen table.

'Give us a dead fly.' He handed them out. Danny Harris, Arthur, Brendan, Davie Martin from next door, John, Archie. The flask felt heavy in the pocket of his shorts but he didn't tell them. At the doorway to the kitchen, he could see Murdo leaning in, having a quiet word in Pinch's ear.

'Time to go, boys.' Mudge, kindly, hands wide. 'Make sure you thank Mr Wilson before you go, and Mrs Bell for the cakes.'

They filed inside, Patrick somewhere in the middle, Arthur kicking John's heels from behind. The hallway was dark, Mudge's congregation waiting patiently to leave, his voice audible in the street outside. Ahead was Pinch Wilson, smiling at a middle-aged lady, was that the Russian woman? Two kids scampered past, 'Thanks Mr Wilson', and out into the grey sunshine. Around my nine-year-old father tall men were putting on hats and smiles. In the narrow corridor, the doorway offered the only bright spot, until Murdo McLean moved across it to shake hands with a man in a brown suit. Behind, Patrick heard Davie Martin sigh at the blocked escape route. Now two away from the door, Patrick could hear Pinch talking to a thin lady whose tights sagged like the skin on old custard. In his pocket, the flask felt clammy and cold.

'Thanks Mr Wilson.'

'Any time, Patrick.' Pinch Wilson leaned down to shake his hand and Patrick could see the blotches and bumps on his jaw. It looked like a road that hadn't been rolled flat yet, something not finished, not entirely civilised. Wilson kept hold of his hand and Patrick had a terrible feeling that he could smell the metal on his skin.

'You want something, you let me know.' Pinch smiled, and his lips drew back from his teeth. 'Any time.'

The other boys were waiting for him by the kerb, beside the Jaguar. Davie joined them after a moment and as they turned to walk home, or play football, or share the Rich Tea biscuits which Danny and Arthur had stuffed in their pockets, Patrick looked back and saw Murdo watching them.

That was the last parish party my father attended at Pinchbeck Wilson's, he told me. He never used the hip flask, never told a soul until today, he said. It was March and he was dying and though there were robins and thrushes singing in the bony trees, his breath formed thin clouds, each wisp one fewer.

He thought it would feel different, he said, sweet as a mug of tea with too many sugars. Not to take what Pinch offered, but to steal it. When he got home though, he was afraid. Afraid of his father and his one warning, afraid of the German entrenching tool, afraid of Pinchbeck Wilson and the menace of 'any time'.

He felt the eye of Murdo McLean on his back and when he swallowed, he tasted metal.

Mark's Fortunes: A Story in Nine Parts
Laura Williams

One. Mark is pissed on by a dog.

A dog has been running around the scrubby grass of Leicester Square Gardens since Mark and his friends arrived. At first, it tries to eat the scraps of their Burger King burgers before turning its attention to another group of tourists. Mark's teenage girlfriend watches as it hungrily takes ice cream cones from their hands. A couple of shirtless labourers, soaking up hazy rays, taunt the dog when it tries to eat their sandwiches. None of Marks' friends notice when the dog trots up to Mark, sniffs his back and cocks its leg. They hear the piss hitting his bomber jacket before he feels it soaking through. His reaction – jumping up and swearing – is slightly delayed, and the reaction of his friends – laughing loud schoolgirl laughs – doesn't happen immediately either.

*

Two. Mark is pissed off by a dog.

'Fuck!' Mark shouts. 'Fuck.' He shouts again. The schoolgirls continue to laugh.

He looks around for the dog to kick it but it has already dashed out of the gardens. He struggles out of his sodden jacket and throws it to the ground. Its highly flammable interior has done little to absorb any of the liquid. There is a large wet patch on his t-shirt which he cranes his neck over his shoulder to see.

'Fuck!' He shouts again.

His friends remain seated on the grass, looking up at him, disgusted, as if it were his fault that a dog decided to piss on him rather than the leg of a bench or the base of a tree.

Three. Where can you buy a t-shirt in Leicester Square?

They all go to a tourist stall selling shot glasses with tube station branding. Sun-faded postcards – of Lady Di and of breasts with mice drawn on them – are displayed tidily. The stall owner closely observes the gaggle of five girls and Mark.

'Have you got…' one girl asks the stallholder as she looks at the t-shirts on display. 'Have you got one that says 'I went to London and got pissed on by a dog and this was the only lousy t-shirt I could buy'?'

*

Four. At his girlfriend's house later the same day.

'I really like your t-shirt, Mark,' says the girl's mum. 'Are you quite new to London?'

'Not really,' Mark replies. 'I ran away from my family in Wales several years ago.'

'Oh,' says the mum. 'Would you like some Tizer?'

*

Five. Mark gets a flat.

Mark doesn't like to spend too much time in his flat. He can feel the chill of the concrete beneath the thin wooden floors. The magnolia walls are bare and the lighting is dim in some rooms and fluorescent in others. There is a lot of space for just him. Cans of beans sit forgotten in kitchen cupboards.

Mark only sleeps in the flat when there is no other option: when the doorways are too cold or when there is enough Special Brew in his system to make him pass out on his bed.

If he is awake in the day, Mark prefers to get off the itchy settee and go outside. He wanders around the local area, catching up with a few people here and there, looking for a bit of cash in hand work.

*

Six. Mark carries a scaffolding pole along a South London street.

Mark is no longer going out with the teenage girl. She

dumped him when she started her 'A' levels. One day, when he is carrying a scaffolding pole from one end of the street to the other to earn some cash, Mark bumps into one of her friends. Mark notices that she's grown up a lot since he last saw her.

'What you doing these days?' she asks.

Mark is still holding the scaffolding pole. 'Not much,' he replies. 'How's Katy?'

'She got fat. Really fat. She drives to the bus stop to go to college.'

'Oh,' Mark replies.

He continues his journey up the road.

*

Seven. Mark remembers his first kiss.

Mark is fourteen. She is in a polka dot dress and has curly hair and a singsong Welsh accent that is rarely heard on Mark's estate.

'Can I walk you to the bus stop?' he asks.

They walk hand in hand. Mark is quite short, shorter than her.

'There won't be a bus for fifteen minutes,' she says. 'Shall we wait under that tree?'

It is a big tree. Mark imagines himself pushing her against it and kissing her. She imagines the same and gets there first. He doesn't mind because standing on the slope around the bottom of the tree makes him taller than her.

He shuts his eyes and enjoys the kiss. It goes on for a while and they move around in their embrace. As he breathes through his nose he catches an unpleasant smell that is unmistakable. The vinegary shit of dogs fed on cheap food. She smells it too and scrunches up her nose.

'Ugh,' she says, pulling away from him.

She runs off down the hill to the bus stop.

Mark drags his feet home.

*

Eight. Mark goes to a children's party.

Mark is a child. He is nine. He has been invited to Joanne Edwards' birthday party. The year before, as an iced gem craze swept the school, Joanne's mum had impressed her classmates by buying bags and bags of the miniature biscuits with colourful icing. With plenty to go around, the children ignored the crisps, jelly and sandwiches as they stuffed handful after handful of iced gems into their mouths. One girl was sick in her own Wellington boots. Joanne's ninth party was very much looked forward to, even by the boys who said she smelt and the girls who pulled her hair.

Mark lives across the road from Joanne. On the day of her party, he watches through the window as the other children begin to arrive.

'Can I go to Joanne's now?' He calls to his mum who always insists on seeing him across the street. As usual, she is in no hurry to get changed out of her dressing gown. She is sitting in the garden, smoking.

'Don't know why you're in such a rush to get over there,' she shouts back. 'Whole bloody family smells of piss.'

She smokes another cigarette and slowly gets dressed. Still wearing her slippers, she walks him across the road. At the front gate she gives him a kiss and whispers 'hold your nose.'

Inside, he follows Joanne's mum into the kitchen. As he adds his gift to the pile, Joanne's Gran tells the other adults sitting in a haze of cigarette smoke that Mark is Joanne's boyfriend. They laugh. Mark blushes and shakes his head. They laugh again. A kitten eats ice cream out of a tub on the table. Joanne comes into the kitchen, holding out a red plastic bowl and asking for more jelly and ice cream.

Mark goes into the other room.

'Have an iced gem,' the other children say.

'Eat one at the same time as some pineapple and cheese,' one suggests, 'Or a twiglet.'

Mark picks out a violet frosted biscuit. It is slightly damp and he thinks of the kitten in the kitchen. He decides that he doesn't want anything else to eat in Joanne Edwards' house. He looks out of the window and can see into his own living room. It glows with the television and he imagines his mum, back in her dressing gown, chuckling away at a Saturday quiz show. It will be two hours before she will be back to collect him.

*

Nine. Mark gets a job in Toys R Us.

Mark works at the Toys R Us on the Old Kent Road. The name badge machine is broken, so he wears one left behind by an employee who was caught cutting the paws off teddy bears. The staff call Mark 'Derek'. He stacks stuffed dogs and dolls made in China.

Kids come to the store to browse after school. They steal more than they buy. One rainy October Tuesday, a group of eleven year olds show up. They knock down a display of Buzz Lightyears and laugh at Mark when he picks them up.

'Look,' one of them says, pointing at Mark. 'Look, it's Geoffrey.'

They all laugh.

'Oi, Geoffrey.' They all shout at him. 'Sing the song to us, Geoffrey. Oi, Geoffrey.'

Mark stands up and chases them onto the Old Kent Road. 'My name is not fucking Geoffrey,' he shouts after them. 'It's Mark.'

Keep Calm and Carry On
Katy Darby

The announcement came right in the middle of *The Archers*, which was, of course, typical. There was a not-entirely-coincidental storyline about impending war and what to do with the livestock if the bomb dropped, and all of a sudden Charlotte Green's comforting, recorded voice came on:

'We interrupt this programme with an emergency announcement. Early-warning systems have detected a number of nuclear missiles heading for Southern England. Please retire to your fallout shelters with your radios and await further instructions.'

It was a feeling of relief more than anything, I suppose. After all, everyone had been talking about and around it for so long; it had to happen some time. Not that it was a self-fulfilling prophecy, exactly. It's just that things with the Americans had got so bad, there was really no way out of it. Still, best to get it over with and just get on with your life, my mother always said.

Or not, as the case might be.

To be quite honest, it didn't make an awful lot of difference to me at my age, especially having lived through a war before. I was used to bombs and sleeping in the cellar and eating out of tins and all that sort of thing. In fact it was rather nostalgic for me – brought the good old days flooding back, especially the tins of Spam. I had plenty of cans and boxes (cat-food and people food) and enough Highland Spring to last for three weeks, even though it was generally agreed that two weeks was quite enough for the lethal radiation levels to drop.

I hurried into the kitchen and scooped up Charles and Camilla, one under each arm. They yowled in surprise, then flopped obediently as I marched down the stairs to the cellar. I went back upstairs to collect my emergency survival bag (passport, spare reading glasses, a thousand pounds in twenties and my heart pills) and made it back down again with a minute to spare before the sirens started going off.

The cellar was just as I'd left it: camp bed, comfy chair, curtained-off washing area, litter tray, a dozen Catherine Cooksons nearly-new from Oxfam, and one whole wall of food, water, batteries and other essentials. I sat on the chair with Charles and Camilla firmly clamped on my lap and closed my eyes. The wailing of the sirens took me right back to when I was a girl, sheltering in Aldwych Station as the Luftwaffe droned overhead. It was quite soothing, actually, and I nodded off with no trouble at all.

*

I'll pass over the next fortnight on the grounds that it was extremely dull and, after the chemical toilet stopped working on Day Ten, rather unpleasant. Camilla and Charles kept me company, of course, but I must say that time dragged rather. I missed my usual routines – chatting with Elsie at Oxfam, visiting the Day Centre, Pay What You Can night at the Thai restaurant in the High Street. The little things.

So when Day Fourteen came I couldn't wait to get out of the cellar. The nearest thing I had to a radiation suit was a pair of salopettes from the Seventies, one of Bernie's leather jackets (also from the Seventies) and his old motorcycle helmet. I must have looked a right sight as I staggered out of the front door into the dusty sunshine, but better safe than sorry, as mother always said.

The first thing I noticed was that there wasn't much damage at all to our part of London, although I could see in the distance that both the Gherkin and the Post Office Tower had crumbled and most of the West End was a smoking crater. But there were really hardly any bodies in the street, and most of them were quite fresh. I supposed they were the impatient ones who'd sneaked out of their shelters early, hoping to be the first looters on the scene. They would have caught a lot of alpha and beta particles, depending on how long they'd left it: it wasn't a very nice way to go, but at least they weren't rotting yet.

Camilla had elected to stay in the basement, but Charles followed close at my heels as I shuffled down the road, making for the corner shop. I still had plenty of Spam and beans left, but I fancied a bit of variety and I was reasonably sure that Pot Noodles would taste the same whether they'd been irradiated or not. Also, I needed some more catfood. And I was rather hoping that Mohammed would be able to tell me what was going on with the infrastructure, because if I couldn't get a bus to Boots to renew my prescription very soon, I was going to be in trouble.

Unfortunately Mohammed was dead, sprawled over the counter with his head stoved in. He looked like he'd been there for a day or two. Most of the cigarettes and batteries were gone from behind the counter, and all the whisky, vodka and gin. I wondered where Mina and the children were; still in their shelter, probably, waiting for him to come back. They'd be safer there.

I checked my watch and quickly filled my shopper with cat-food, jam and noodles, Charles licking desultorily at the congealed blood on the vinyl floor. Then I hurried back as fast as I could to feed Camilla, whose yowls I could hear half-way down the street. I didn't want attention being drawn to my house, especially if there were gangs about. You can't be too careful, and besides, in times of desperation, people will eat anything – even cats.

I discovered the reason for Camilla's strangled cries when Charles and I returned home; during our absence she had given birth on the camp bed to six tiny sticky kittens, who were already emitting high-pitched mews and tumbling about like Weebles on the bed.

'That bloody vet!' I told her, 'I'll have his guts for garters. He swore to me you'd been neutered.' She just purred weakly. I gave Charles and Camilla their din-dins, spread some plum jam onto a Hob Nob, and settled down for a nap in the comfy chair.

The kittens I decided to christen William and Harry (of course), Beatrice, Eugenie, Diana and Simba. They grew at an alarming rate. Soon the corner shop ran out of catfood, and I had to start giving my little royal family beans and Spam. Then the beans and Spam ran out, and I was forced to start thinking seriously about how on earth I was going to get to the High Street for more supplies without getting mugged or keeling over.

The situation was urgent now, you see: I'd taken the last of my spare, emergency-only heart pills several days ago and if I couldn't get to Boots things didn't look good for me. There were, needless to say, no buses (no change there, to be quite honest) so I stumped slowly down the street trying the doors of all the cars. Bernie had taught me to hotwire our old VW in the Sixties, when he lost the key, and I hoped I still had the knack.

The seventh car was unlocked, and after a bit of fiddling about, I got it started. It was only a ten-minute drive to the High Street, but it was still very eerie not to see a single other car on the road all the way there. When I drove up and parked in front of Boots I saw that the front windows had been smashed in: lipstick and face cream lay scattered over the floor, but the entire snack section and the pharmacy at the back had been swept completely clean.

In vain I picked through the few intact bottles on the floor; but there was nothing of any use, nothing for me and my heart; all gone, to sell or trade or take. Paracetamol, Oil of Evening Primrose and Viagra were all that was left. I took them anyway. Just in case.

'Oh Charles,' I said softly, 'We are in a bit of a pickle.'

The pickle got worse as I drove back down along the High Street, assessing the damage. No shop was intact, not even the tanning salon; not even the undertaker's (although I suppose that made some sort of sense). The pet shop had burned down. The Budgens was a wreckage of blood and broken glass, and even Holland and Barrett had been raided; the shelves of organic rice cakes and Panda liquorice bars standing clean and empty. No food anywhere, for cats or people.

Charles and I drove back home in silence. Fifty yards from the house, the car's engine gave out.

Down in the cellar, I checked my dwindling stock of tins. Some chickpeas, a can or two of spinach and rather a lot of Bird's Custard – nothing the cats would touch. Camilla, William and Simba wove themselves thickly between my legs, purring loudly, waiting to be fed. The little ones were nearly as big as their parents, now; strong and hungry.

I remembered something I'd read or seen, years ago, a Cold War documentary which had mentioned some of the creatures that can survive nuclear aftermath with no ill-effects. Cockroaches would be all right, I knew that much. And so would rats. I didn't recall them saying anything about cats. I suppose the cats could eat the rats, eventually, but what if they couldn't find any, or catch them if they did? What if they needed to build up their strength first, to be taught how to hunt? What would they live on until then?

I was still pondering this dilemma as I finished a frugal meal of Hob Nobs and custard and reached to the bookshelf, only to find that I had read my last Catherine Cookson. I stopped, staring at my hand – old, gnarled, and trembling, the veins raised over the bony knuckles, shiny and purple like worms. I suddenly felt breathless, and my heart started jumping and thudding. It felt like a pair of kittens was wrestling in my ribcage.

And then I realised what was probably the best thing to do, what with my heart pills gone, and Boots cleaned out, and the car broken down, and the world ending and all. I put my warm cardy on, because the evening was getting a bit nippy and the cellar always was rather damp.

Then I poured myself a tot of brandy and took the bottle of little blue diamond-shaped pills out of my pocket. NOT TO BE TAKEN BY PERSONS WITH HEART CONDITIONS, it said on the side, in large black letters. *That'll do*, I thought, and downed five of them.

As I waited for the pills to take effect, the cats gathered round me, leaping onto my lap, draping themselves over my feet; watching, waiting, purring, almost as if they knew. I was fairly sure it wouldn't take them too long to get the idea, once I'd gone cold. As the only source of food in a hungry world, my body, scrawny though it was, would feed them all for a good few weeks, and that would give them an advantage out there, against the rats and the cockroaches and whatever else had survived.

I hoped my little ones all would all find good homes. I comforted myself with the thought that people would need cats more than ever once they started rebuilding society or whatever it was one did in a post-Apocalyptic nightmare future which I, for one, was rather glad I wasn't going to live to see.

'Waste not, want not,' my mother always said.

And I won't. And they shan't.

Leaving
Cherry Potts

Friday: lunchtime. In the pub, getting drunk. Goodbye drink –
have another – leaving work.

Sitting crushed into the corner of a table-for-ten at the
Tiger. Feeling slightly sick. Always hated leaving dos. Two too
many gins.

Been here over an hour already, the others come and go
in shifts – someone has to keep the office open. We'll all be ill
by half past three.

Not really listening to their chatter; no need, they
aren't talking to me, as though I've already gone. Anticipating
freedom, my pulse is racing, waiting to be on the train, waiting
to go home, waiting to leave.

Won't work this afternoon, just sit and listen to them talk
– 'All the best Allie darling,' (I bet) – and how much they'll miss
me (not much). At least they'll be talking to *me*, not like now.

Jane said she'd come over for a quick one. Knew she
wouldn't though. Saving her strength for the goodbye speech.
Hope it's not a cut glass fruit bowl – that's what they gave the
last person who left.

They don't know what my new job is yet. Tell them just
before I go, when I've got the cut glass fruit bowl – or maybe not.

I'm wearing my pink jacket with the triangles woven
into it.

'That's a pretty colour Allie darling, I must get one like
that. Isn't it a pretty pattern, don't you think so Sue? Where
d'you get it?'

Gary's got me another drink – if I swallow it I'll throw up.
Give it to Jenny. She, the responsible one, looks at her watch –
what a relief, it's time we all went back – but she has to justify

breaking up the party:

'Her upstairs will be complaining.' (Jane she means.)

Jane knows about the job, she wrote the reference, after all. Bet that's why she didn't come to the pub. She's been a bit standoffish since. Thought she'd understand... thought she understood.

We stagger back to the office, a giggling straggling gaggle.

Gary nearly got run over – dead funny that. Won't miss that road.

The office is stuffy with illicit cigarette smoke; the heating is up too high. The phone rings unanswered while they eat the cream cakes, supplied by me.

Suddenly feel very sick.

Hiding in the ladies, I rest my head on the ice-cold tiles, wishing it were over, wishing I didn't have to go back into that noisy drunken crowd.

I hate them. Can afford to admit it, now I don't have to be with them day in, day out.

Go back to find them waiting in proper groups for me.

'The queen is on her way downstairs,' says Jenny, 'I hope you remember to curtsy.'

Used to like Jenny. Might even miss her a little, but not her constant sniping.

Sit down in my corner, trying not to laugh; it must be all those gins – Jane pretends she hasn't noticed, gives us all her mechanical smile.

'Are we all ready?' she asks, obliging. Confidence oozes from every clean-cut line of her, success from every stitch. (Sue got a jacket just like that one – up the market, fifty quid.)

I stand next to her, both with practised smiles – she makes occasional jokes – no one laughs. They all hate her anyway.

'I'm sure we all wish Allie the best of luck at...'

I crush her toe with a weighty heel; No, suddenly I really don't want her to tell them. She gets the message.

'...Her new place of work,' through gritted teeth. I move my foot. She thrusts a small parcel into my hand, doesn't quite let go, so her fingers press mine in passing.

'Thank you, at least it's not a fruit bowl'; they laugh uncertainly.

'Go on open it – no one's seen it 'cept Jane,' Sue demands, all impatient curiosity.

'I chose it,' Jane explains, catching my eye.

Open the box, look inside, shut it quick. They look expectant, but I'm not going to satisfy their curiosity.

Silence. Jane shakes my hand, and goes.

Watch her retreating, shoulders slumping. Oh God.

'What is it then?'

'Where are you going, Allie?'

Ignore their starling like clamour, grab my coat.

'Home,' I say, fiercely indifferent. They scatter before me, confused, surprised.

Catch her in the corridor.

She turns and smiles. A real smile; just for me.

'Quite a leap of faith,' she says.

I stare blankly.

'The job,' she says impatient, 'I wish I had your nerve. It's really taking being out at work to extremes.'

Almost sounds like criticism. Could be jealousy. Try my best not-a-care-in-the world grin. (Actually, terrified; this hated, despised place actually looks safe right now... hey, she doesn't need to know).

'I'll be right at home.'

Nooo, did that sound aggressive? Didn't mean... Shouldn't drink gin at lunchtime.

'I hope you like it,' she says cheerfully. Wonder if she means the job or the small silver symbol still clutched in my hand, wrapped in a bit of paper.

'I hope you'll use it,' she says, less sure of herself this time.

Wonder if she means the pendant or the phone number that encloses it.

'Oh ... yes,' ...calculating the time of the next Lewisham-bound train, suddenly embarrassed, feeling I have, after all, mistaken her. If I run, I'll just catch it and be home in…

'Allie.' Her voice wobbles, even on that short word – she's staring hard at the wall.

Honestly, I despair of her.

Why does she think I'm leaving?

Take her hand; let the train go without me.

Incurable Romantic Seeks Dirty Filthy Whore
Martin Pengelly

Leaning, against the wind, on the concrete brim of a water feature in the middle of the Brunswick Centre's concrete plaza, Henson scratched his recently-bearded chin. Spray, whipped by the breeze, dotted his cheek. Honoria the Dentist was late; the film started in five minutes.

Well, the ads started in five minutes, after the lights dimmed and the screen glowed briefly, an enormous Rothko. And then there were the trailers, ten minutes after the start of the ads. Ten more minutes of trailers, then, and then the click and hum of the curtains, the pitch into blackness and the BBFC title card. The first chords. So, the film started in twenty-five minutes. Still, Honoria the Dentist was late.

He looked at where his watch should have been, then reached into his pocket for his phone. Twenty-four minutes. But then, he never felt comfortable going into a cinema once the lights were down, whether the screen was showing the first seconds of the new Bertolucci or an advert for sanitary towels. So, four minutes.

He inspected the elbows of his brown corduroy jacket; crossed and re-crossed his legs. Scratched his beard again. Work tomorrow – down the road in Farringdon. Copy. Editing. Saving writers from themselves. Three minutes. Where was she? Henson looked across to the Renoir. Posters: *A Butterfly's Wings Blot Out the Sun*. Chinese. Maoism, Taoism and peasants worrying about getting the water buffalo to market, most likely. Screen Two: *Anna in October*. Charlotte Gainsbourg's erotic underbite. More, much more his thing. The story of a Parisian academic's affair with an English novelist, the autumn after *les évenèments*;

1968 and all that. Messy sex to songs by Françoise Hardy. There was rumoured to be a visible erection, but he'd missed it the first time he saw the film.

Nor had he clocked the cock, as it were, the second time. Third time lucky, perhaps. He looked again at his phone. Two minutes. No Dentist. Outside Starbucks, people slurped Frappuccinos and sucked cigarettes.

He'd first seen *Anna in October* two weeks ago. Its first day out. On his own on a Thursday, a day off, unbooked. Scratched about on his novel in the morning – an epic about war artists written, he thought, by a piss artist – then took the tube to town for a coffee and a sandwich at the London Review Bookshop. Gazed in dumb awe at the Israeli PhD who worked the Gaggia with a long-limbed languor that spoke, to him, of kibbutzim and refuseniks and being nice to Palestinians. Not that it mattered – for her, he'd turn Zionist. Raised, eventually, from his rapture, he'd walked down the side of the Museum and across Russell Square. Went home after the film to read it up in *Sight & Sound* and go, after pasta, to bed.

One minute. No Dentist. He thought of his companion for viewing number two, last week: Carolina from the Comment Desk, a bespectacled Yank beauty with a chest. An old girlfriend who worked across the office. She'd asked if he fancied *Anna in October*, as no one she knew wanted to see it. They'd walked up after work; eaten sushi at a chain outlet and watched the film. Both, it turned out, missed the fabled erection. Going home, Henson's own scarcely glimpsed, once fabled erection subsided as he passed through Stockwell. The hope of sex for old time's sake, perhaps inspired by Charlotte Gainsbourg's exertions, had died during a stilted conversation on the walk to Warren Street.

No minutes. That was it, then. The Dentist was late and they were missing the start of the film. Damn it. Where the hell was she? Could there be that many molars in the world?

A female voice. He didn't look up.

'Peter! Over here!'

He looked up. Holding the cinema door, waving; hooped earrings wafting in the breeze. Brown hair in a scallop-shell clip. Susannah the Mad Christian. He stared.

'Peter! Come on, we're missing the start of the film!'

In the beginning there was darkness, and out of darkness came the truth and the light. And though it passed all understanding, Henson saw he'd made a mistake. Susannah the Mad Christian. Not Honoria the Dentist. He was seeing the film with Susannah the Mad Christian. The cataloguing system, the taxonomy, was supposed to prevent such errors. Offering a silent prayer for forgiveness – may the Dentist drill in peace, may she accidentally flick a nerve and instruct me to rinse for all eternity – he jogged over to the cinema.

'I've been in there half an hour, you silly,' said Susannah, with a pout. Henson reflected on the use of 'silly' as an honorific. 'So I've bought the tickets. Come on!'

He trotted meekly down the stairs.

*

During the film, as Charlotte Gainsbourg argued with a German in a rumpled corduroy suit, Henson remembered the last time he'd dated Susannah the Mad Christian. She'd caught God – napping, presumably – in the space between their first relationship and their second. He doubted there would be a third, given that the second had ended with an argument in bed, where sex, at which he knew her to be a surprisingly aerobatic adept, had been withheld. The argument was about her new-found faith. She'd asked him to respect it. He'd said he respected her, but not it. Then – he might have fought his way out of that one – he'd made his fatal mistake. Quoting Josef Goebbels, he knew now, was never a good idea. Never. In fact, selectively misquoting him ('you know, Susannah, as Goebbels said, when I hear the word 'religion' I reach for my gun') was probably worse. Susannah the Mad Christian had thrown on her clothes and stormed out. He'd waved goodbye from the window.

This evening had come about thanks to a meeting at a party in Clapham and the revelation that Susannah, now speaking to him again, didn't know anyone else who would go to see a foreign film. Did he want to see *Anna in October*? He thought of a night in a ground-floor flat in Leytonstone, and agreed.

After the film, they walked to Tottenham Court Road so she could get back to Acton, where the missionary work was arduous. Perhaps the natives were restless, or just not particularly Baptist. In Henson's mind, Charlotte Gainsbourg strode across the Pont Neuf, on her way to a rendezvous with the English novelist, who was played by a chap he'd seen in *Richard II* at the Globe. At the bottom of the escalators, Susannah the Mad Christian, whom he hadn't dared ask about the erection, which he'd missed again, shook his hand – *shook his hand* – and ran off to the Central Line.

So, he thought, as the train stopped at Kennington and he joined an irritable throng on the next platform, there would now be Honoria the Dentist. He supposed there would always be Honoria the Dentist, whom he'd met at another party, the same weekend. Privately educated, red-blonde. About six foot. Teeth like tombstones. He'd asked her out for a drink. She'd suggested the cinema: there was a film, *Anna in October,* which she couldn't persuade anyone to see. He'd said he'd seen it but no, really, he'd only end up hanging about in a gallery if they didn't. So they'd made a date – for next Thursday. Well.

*

Next Thursday, at the Renoir, Honoria the Dentist paid for the sushi and Henson got the tickets. The whey-faced student in the bullet-proof box seemed to nod in recognition; he gave her a wan smile. After the film, on the walk to Russell Square, the Dentist enthused about the German, whom Henson had recently seen playing a good Nazi in a Dutch film. As aspiring British actors did pub Shakespeare and appeared in The Bill, so their Teutonic equivalents stuck on a cap and jackboots and played Hitler with a conscience.

He took hold of her hand. For one, awful moment it hung there, lifeless. Then it dropped away and the Dentist earnestly told him that though she'd had such a good time, and had enjoyed the film awfully, they really mustn't try to force anything, must they? He agreed and, in desperation, started cracking jokes. Tube light, he discovered under a slightly withering gaze – no, she hadn't seen the promised erection either – was particularly harsh. The Dentist looked rather severe, here. God knew what it did to him. He could feel beads of sweat at his temples by Clapham Common, where she pecked his cheek and departed.

*

The next Monday, sitting on his concrete seat, he waited for another date. He wondered about Honoria the Dentist. She'd turned the situation, effortlessly. All he'd done was slip her hand into his, and after five minutes he'd felt like some kind of peasant. Perhaps it was just as well that they were now to meet, next week, 'as friends'. What with bowing and scraping being so inconvenient during sex, and all.

His date, Alexia the Actress, a curvy blonde with cheekbones and problems with her father, rather surprisingly missed the erection – and looked a little shocked when he mentioned it, having missed it too. Alexia had slept with Henson once, ages ago, and hadn't objected to his choice of film, but she spent the drink before and the sushi after asking why his friend Ben didn't like her and removing his hand from her thigh. Three days later, Tilda the Desk Editor – much older, and Spanish – said yes, of course she'd seen the erection. Hadn't he? Then she went home to her husband.

In the end despair won out and Henson, mindful of *Anna in October*'s departure to a couple of nights at the Prince Charles and then DVD, rang Meriel the History Teacher. She – two years older, two months together two years ago and occasional, rather too fraught emails since – turned up wearing a suede jacket, a corduroy skirt, sensible tights and a hopeful expression. They ate sushi. The film flicked by and Henson, slumped in his seat, mouthed along to Charlotte Gainsbourg's final monologue. The English novelist killed himself – she wrote a bestselling sociological treatise and moved in with the German. The End. He put Meriel the History Teacher on the Circle Line at Euston Square. She cried.

*

Two weeks later, Henson's phone rang. It was, he saw, Emma the Duplicitous Ex. A honey-haired, green-eyed beauty. Five months together five years ago, including an anatomically exhausting weekend in a cheap Montmartre hotel and ill-advised use of the word 'love'. She must be back from Kabul, where she'd gone shortly after they'd last had coffee on the Buckingham Palace Road. Oddly, she wasn't the first person who, on gaining his attentions, had promptly gone to work in a war zone. Still, here she was, in the country and, evidently, not yet back in the arms of Michael the Quantity Surveyor – the boyfriend she'd had, it turned out, the whole time. He'd been in China, Henson remembered. Probably worrying about getting the water buffalo to market. Then he'd come back and Emma the Duplicitous Ex had gone to live with him. Once, playing rugby, Henson had been kicked, hard, in the testicles. That about covered it.

He pressed 'answer'. Emma the Duplicitous Ex asked if he wanted to go to the cinema. The Renoir, in fact.

He suppressed a groan. It couldn't be back, could it? *Anna in October*? Again?

Not that. Not sushi, not another heap of dead tuna. Not another bottled beer, another ninety minutes sat next to middle-aged men in architects' specs. Not another earnest conversation on the walk to the tube. Not – oh, please – not no sex. Again.

He'd stood at Serge Gainsbourg's grave once, in

Montparnasse. 'Well, Serge,' he'd said, to no one in particular. 'I think I fancy your daughter almost as much as you did.'

Not any more, he didn't.

He cleared his throat. His heart sank.

'It's a special,' said Emma the Duplicitous Ex. 'Pasolini's anniversary. *120 Days of Sodom.*'

He arranged to meet her at seven.

Red
David Mildon

May 29th '85

The phone is ringing. Footsteps on the stairs. Mum whispering. Silence. Footsteps on the stairs. My bedroom door opening and Mum's on top of me, tears on her face and in her curls and on me. Holding me too tight.

When I catch my breath, I ask 'What was the score?' She pulls back, looks at me, looks at Kenny Dalglish above my bed, the scarves and the rosettes, all red.

'Dad's safe. The rest doesn't matter.'

February 17th '87

It's cold by the Cutty Sark, the wind finding ways through my duffelcoat. Mum is fiddling with the camera, trying to get a photo. She likes to do this. My Dad always asks why she can't just remember things. As he's not here yet, I make the familiar observation in his place.

'Because I want a photo.'

'It's cold.'

'And? Look, just stand still and try to smile for once.'

'Why should I? It's…'

And suddenly I'm rising through the air, a hand under each armpit. My legs draped over my father's shoulders.

'Are you gonna stop making your mam's life a misery and smile? Eh, monkey boy?'

Of course, now I'm beaming.

'Give us the pamphlets Paul.'

Reluctantly my father hands her the red and yellow leaflets emblazoned with 'DEIRDRE WOOD FOR MP'. As Mum turns to put them in her bag, he slaps a sticker with the same message on my lapel, giving me a confidential smile.

The photo taken, we head back north of the Thames, Dad handing out leaflets as we go.

'Vote for Deirdre Wood'

'Vote for Deirdre Wood'

'Vote for Deirdre Wood'

And then.

'Fuck off.'

Two young men, just out of boyhood, in front of us now, all denim and snarls.

Down from my dad's shoulders and into my mum's arms. Her hurrying me away. My father standing his ground.

'You shouldn't talk like that son.'

'I'm not your fucking son.'

An echoing melee of arms and feet and just Dad standing. Looking down at the two. Head bowed as if ashamed, but his eyes shining.

Deirdre Wood lost the election. But Dad won the fight. Red for Liverpool FC, red for Labour. Scouse.

April 5th 1987

Tying my laces again and again. Just my Stan Smiths, not football boots, but all the pre-match rituals are in place. Because today I'm not playing, I'm watching. The Mighty Reds. London born, but no question who my team was going to be. Dad's team. Dad's city. Liverpool. A good breakfast. Mum lays out the Full English for 'her two men'. I'm wearing the Crown Paints sponsored shirt. The one we won the double in. Jacket on, hat on, scarf on.

Dad stops me in the front hall. Takes the hat off, the scarf off. Zips up my jacket so the shirt's covered up.

'Going to a game son. You and I both know who you're cheering for, don't we?'

And we're off. Walk to the station. Dad's telling me about Jimmy Case, Kevin Keegan and John Toshack. The sun's shining. British Rail. Battersea Power Station arcing off to the right. Ray Clemence, Emlyn Hughes and Steve Heighway. Down into the Underground and the singing's echoing through the tunnels. Dad's asking about school. He asks about History, I talk about my friends. They all support West Ham, Spurs and today's opponents: Arsenal. Ours, ours for the asking, ours for the taking.

Into the carriage. Canals of spilt beer run parallel between the slats on the floor. Two stops and we're moving back into the carriage corner with the discarded beer-cans at our feet. A wave of men. Filling the train with noise, smell and red and white. Scarves on wrists, shirts out, hands clapping, confident in numbers. Arsenal.

Dad looks down smiling, sees my face, winks and puts a hand on my shoulder.

Every handle is in motion now, batted in time against the side of the train, the springs flying back and forth:

And it's Super Gunners,

Super Arsenal FC,

We'll play the world over,

And champions we'll be!!

Beer sprayed further down the carriage, people getting off, getting away. I look up. Dad still wears his serene smile.

Next stop, a boy gets on with his father. He's got the scarf, the sweatbands and the bobble hat. All red. His tight shiny Liverpool shirt is oozed over the rolls of his jumper: warm and red, without losing one or the other.

It's gone quiet in the carriage. The father, quiet too, taking up exactly the space a man needs with his son close. No more, but certainly no less. Casually holding on to a sprung handle; he knows the Tube because he's looking calmly at his son, which shows he doesn't need to check the map for the route to Wembley.

And then it starts. All the men are singing. I know the song; hear it on TV and when Uncle Pat is here at Christmas. This time the words are different.

Sign on,
Sign on,
With a pen in your hand,
Cos you'll never get,
A job,
A job,
You'll neeeevuh get a job.

The boy's face is flushed. They're too close to him. My face is flushed too, but no-one's looking at me. They're close. No-one's moved but they're closer. One man, just one, kneels down amid the beer streams and the fag-ends. Looking quizzically at the surprise and confusion painted on the boy's face. Then up at the lad's father, then back to him.

Dad's stopped smiling.

The man's now eye to eye with the boy, but still no closer and I realise he's waiting for the singers to stop. Then loudly but slowly, with a coaxing smile as one song stops, he starts singing:

You are a scouser,
A dirty scouser,
You're only happy on giro day,
Your dad's been stealing,
Your mum's drug-dealing,
So please don't take my hub-caps away ... away!

Now they're all singing, it's rolling up and down the carriage like an echo but echoes get quieter and this doesn't.

The boy looks up at his father. Without a word or comment, the father's hand curves on the boy's shoulder, gently arcing him round and away because we've pulled in to another station.

The doors open, the boy's feet are on neutral ground,

provoking a fusillade of hand wanking and swear-words from inside the train. The boy stays looking through the window as the door closes, looking straight through the crowd at my Dad. Still looking as the train pulls out of the station.

My Dad looks away first. His hand tight on my shoulder. His eyes on the floor.

Arsenal won two-one.

Palio
Liam Hogan

'How does it work?'

I slide the sheet of paper over without looking up from my game of patience. 'Like the Palio in Siena? Eight departments, or 'Contrada', represented by eight runners. Three circuits of the office, starting and ending at the lifts by Reception.'

'And who are the runners?'

'It's on the list.'

'But not the odds?'

'There aren't any.' I sigh, bored of explaining. 'Apart from a bottle of fizz for the runner, the winners divide the pot – the more you put in, the bigger slice you get back.'

'And it's really going to happen? How are you going to get away with it?' He asks doubtfully.

'There's an offsite for the managers this afternoon.' I reply. 'But that just affords the opportunity. I'm not going to get away with it – it's my last day here, which is why I ask for the money up-front.' I add pointedly.

'Ah, yes.' He has the decency to look slightly uncomfortable, though I'm not sure whether it's sympathy for me or embarrassment at being told to flash his cash. Then he reaches for a wallet that could choke a pony and slips out a brightly coloured note. 'On Matt Beasley, for the FX traders. See you in the pub afterwards?'

I nod briefly. Fifty quid? The smug git. Canny though, Beasley was in the TA, and with a few overturned wastepaper baskets, it could turn into an assault course. Not that it really mattered. Not the way I was playing the game.

I wouldn't have minded redundancy. I was only working until I had enough for my trip round the world, and three months paid leave would have suited me down to the ground. But because I'd not worked at Darkwood Capital Management for a full year, they didn't need to make me redundant, did they? Instead, I was told I was definitely being let go, but only after I'd worked my full notice period. Nice.

I make my way over to Reception. When the last of the managers leave, Emmeline has agreed to parade a banner bearing the symbols of the eight Contrada round the course to let everyone know the race is about to begin. Only, she isn't there.

'Ah... she popped out for a smoke. She's a bit nervous.' Claire says.

'Emmeline? Nervous?' Every hedge fund seems to have at least one singular beauty at Reception, there to smile for the Investors and add a bit of glamour to the disappointing returns. Ours was Emmeline. I wouldn't have thought she was the sort to get butterflies.

'Yes...' Claire nods. 'And to tell you the truth, so am I.'

'Oh, you'll be fine I'm sure.' I smile warmly. Claire was one of the runners, representing all the little teams, like the receptionists, that weren't big enough to form a department.

She tilts her head to one side and shrugs. 'It's not the race I'm worried about.'

I lean over the counter. 'It's only a bit of fun.' I say. 'This place has been like a morgue since the redundancies. Where's the harm? We're not exactly going to annoy the neighbours – the fourth floor has been empty for three months. Besides, they can't get rid of all of us, can they? And they already got rid of me.'

She bites her lower lip and fiddles with the silver heart on her necklace.

'Besides, I've got ten quid on 'The Chimera'.' I lie. 'So you can't pull out now.'

'Really?' she says, delighted. Claire chose a mythical beast as the symbol for her Contrada. It made an odd sort of sense –

a creature made up of the parts of many others. She was always far too smart to be a receptionist.

'Really.' I grin. 'When Emmeline comes back, let me know, okay?'

'Okay.' She nods. 'And Tony, I'm sorry about … '

I wave my hand dismissively. 'Don't be. I'll land on my feet. I always do.'

There's a flurry of last minute bets that keeps me from finishing my game of patience, but I don't mind. The cash box in my desk drawer is already stuffed with notes, mostly tens and twenties, with a fair few fifties from the traders. I write out each bet on a slip stamped with the Contrada's mascot, and tot up the amounts on a spreadsheet. All very professional. It's neck and neck between Beasley for the Fox, and Alex McAvoy for the Bull, though there's a late surge on Jonson in Legal – for the Eagle – that makes me wonder if there's a fix going in.

At long last the phone rings, and I listen attentively. 'Gents,' I announce, as I replace the handset. 'The race is on. You have until Emmeline comes past to place your bets.'

I collect another fifty quid before Emmeline sashays by, a crowd in tow. I write out the last slip – a tenner on the Stag, and call out 'To the starting line!', while I wait for the printer to churn out the final spreadsheet. By the time I reach Reception there's barely room to squeeze through. I hand the cashbox to Emmeline, and then there's a roar as I hold the bottle of champagne aloft, which only slowly quietens as I continue to hold my stance.

'Ladies and gentleman!' I announce. 'Welcome to the first – and last – Darkwood Office Palio!' I ride the applause and then lift the printout in my hand. 'The bets are in, the runners are ready, and there's absolutely no management anywhere to be seen!'

This time the roar is accompanied by the stamping of feet, and again I wait for hush.

'The Palio is an ancient race, distinguished by its sheer simplicity. The race starts when the tape across the passageway is lowered by the lovely Emmeline.' Wolf whistles cut piercingly across the cheers, and Emmeline gives a mock curtsy. 'Three laps around the perimeter of the office,' I continue, 'Winner takes all, and as for the rules – well, there ARE no rules!' The roar returns with a vengeance.

'But that's for the runners. For the spectators...' I wag my finger, 'Strictly NO interference! Keep off the race course – there's plenty of room between the desks for everyone to get a good view. And we'll need to get a clear route back to Reception before the race can begin. Before you go though, let's introduce the Contradas!'

As I introduce them in order of descending support, each name is met by cheers and jeers in equal measure. 'And last – but by no means least, Claire Fielding for the Chimera!' Claire steps forward, to rapturous applause – more I suspect because I've kept them waiting far too long, rather than last minute support for the official underdog. 'Keep an eye on the tape.' I whisper, and then while I'm still trying to move people aside, I give a quick nod to Emmeline and she drops the red ribbon she's been holding across the corridor. Claire's halfway to the wedged-open door to the trading floor before the other runners notice and as the spectators cheer and holler – I turn and slip quietly into the stairwell.

Although I was only at Darkwood for a little less than a year, there were quite a few leaving dos in that time. I guess the smarter ones got wind of what was coming. And for each of them there was the traditional whip-round. It's funny, the differences in the amounts collected. When a trader left, there would be enough for a flash watch, or a leather briefcase, or an expensive electronic toy. When someone from IT left, they'd barely scrape together enough for a bottle of M&S own brand champagne.

Of course, when a quarter of the staff is made redundant,

there's no time for a whip-round. They were gone the day the announcements were made, drowning their sorrows in the local, wondering what they did wrong, hardly comprehending that the only reason they had been let go was to make the company's bottom line – the ratio between cost and income – look a lot healthier than it really was.

But what about me? As I descend the stairs I wonder if there's a slim envelope somewhere, with a paltry collection of coins that wouldn't even pay for the first round I was expected to buy, and an oversized card partially covered in scrawled 'Good Luck!' messages. I wonder if any of the managers condescended to sign it – the managers whose 'offsite' wasn't very offsite at all – the managers who were in the one functional meeting room on the otherwise unoccupied fourth floor, discussing terms with the prospective new owners, grey accountants from one of the City's more traditional and straight-laced Investment Banks. The managers who had done everything they could to keep the meeting hush-hush, but had still needed help from what remained of IT to set up the projector. The managers who were presumably stood with stormy faces staring up across the central atrium past the glass elevators to the chaos erupting on the fifth floor.

I doubt it. Which is why the cashbox sitting on the Reception desk is full of blank betting slips, and enough coppers to make it rattle; whereas the bulging envelope in my jacket pocket is too full to be sealed shut.

I reach the ground floor and collect my rucksack from building security just as a noise like slow thunder rolls through the building. The guard nods in the direction of the lifts. 'What's happening up there?'

I shrug. 'I don't know. Good news, perhaps.' I'm about to do one last check for my passport and my airline ticket, when I realise I'm still holding the bottle of champagne. I'd like to leave it for Claire, the one decent person in the company, but that would just get her into trouble. I hesitate, and then turn back to the guard. 'Alf, it's my last day here.'

'I'm sorry to hear that, sir,' he says, his voice neutral. I guess he's seen a lot of people come and go. I doubt more than a handful ever bothered to learn his name.

I hand him my security pass, and the bottle. 'For you.' I say with a smile.

The Frog
Emily Cleaver

So, it's Valentine's Day, and this girl, the one this story is about, is walking down the hill from Haringey station to the bus stop on Green Lanes. She works at a bank in the City, but no one knows exactly what she does there. Maybe she doesn't know what she's doing there herself. Anyway. She's walking along, feeling cold and grey as the day because no one's going to send her a Valentine's card. Fog lies like a dirty bed sheet over the valley below, but she's looking at the pavement. Still, that means that she sees the frog, crouching in the gutter among the cigarette butts, splats of spit and discs of chewing gum. At first she thinks someone has dropped a green leather purse, but no. It's a real frog.

The girl stops dead. The sudden silence as her heels stop clacking empties the street. The two rows of boxy houses slip down to the grumbling traffic on the main road. They don't have front gardens, just fences, motorbikes and dead sofas. No ponds, certainly. There is the New River though, running secretly through a brick culvert, between the houses and underneath the street. That must be where the frog has come from.

The girl looks at the frog, and the frog looks back at her. She bends down and picks it up. She doesn't mind the feel of it, because she used to secretly keep frogs slow worms and lizards, in a box under her bed when she was younger. That was before the job at the bank, or the clacking heels, or all this stuff about love and money. The frog's throat flutters and its cold feet pat her palm when it shifts. She shivers. The frog blinks.

'You look sad.'

This is where you can take the story or leave it, depending on your tastes, because it's the frog speaking. Its lips don't move but she can tell by its eyes. Her mouth opens, as if in readiness to receive something on her tongue, but she doesn't say anything, scared suddenly of the empty street listening.

'Put me back in the water, and I will grant your heart's desire.' The frog's voice is chilly.

The girl has many desires in her heart. It's full of them, and not much else. But whatever it is she does in the city, she knows about making deals.

'Which desire?'

'The one at the top. The red one.'

The girl knows that one. It's the one that shadows and stunts the others.

'And I just have to put you back in the water?'

'No, not just that. To repay me you must welcome me into your home, and love me, and feed me from your own plate and let me sleep on your pillow and take me with you wherever you go. I think that's a small price to pay for your heart's most solemn and awful desire.'

There's always the small print, the girl thinks. 'Alright. I will, if you do what you say.'

This isn't a lie when she says it. Whatever it is she does in the city, she's good at making bargains that she means to keep while it suits her.

'Then put me back.'

The girl takes the frog to where the New River ducks under the street and puts her hand through the fence to place him on the grass. He flops into the water and disappears. She can still feel his cold body on the palm of her hand, and the feeling stays there all the way to the bus-stop, and on the bus and all day at the office, as if she is still holding his ghost. And that day at work she meets the man of her dreams, her heart's desire.

'Your hands are cold,' the man of her dreams says to her as

they shake hands, and he smiles a narrow smile.

So, the girl and her deepest darkest heart's desire go out for drinks after work and one thing leads to another and she takes him home. But she takes him a different route, nowhere near the New River. They go to bed, and she discovers his secrets; the line of dark hairs down the centre of his chest, the scar on his thigh, the taste of his narrow mouth. Then, when they are lying there in the dark, her heart's desire fast asleep because he has an early start tomorrow, the girl hears a noise on the stairs up to the door of her flat. Pur-flop. Pur-flop. It's soft as a purse dropping from a pocket. Pur-flop. Pur-flop. It stops outside her door. Flop.

'Open the door. Lift me up to your bed. I have come to sleep on your pillow.'

The girl lies still in the dark, her scalp prickling. She doesn't answer.

'Open the door. I want to lie against your cheek and stay with you wherever you go.'

Her heart's desire shifts in his sleep, but still she doesn't move. She doesn't sleep herself, not that whole long night, or even in the very early morning when she hears the soft pur-flop, pur-flop, moving away down the stairs. She takes the other route to work that day.

At the office, her phone rings, and she almost expects to hear the dank voice of the frog, but it's the man of her dreams, her heart's desire, asking her out for dinner. It's when she goes outside to smoke a cigarette on the pavement that she hears it behind her. Pur-flop. Pur-flop. Louder this time, like rain on tarmac. Pur-flop. Flop.

'Pick me up. You must take me into your office and sit me on your desk.'

The girl doesn't turn around, just blows a jet of smoke upwards.

'Pick me up. I want to come with you everywhere. I want to watch you work.'

She drops her cigarette and grinds it under her toe, then she goes back inside.

At the restaurant, her heart's desire, the man of her dreams, buys her a bright red rose in a plastic sheath. She returns his narrow smile, and raises her voice when she thanks him, but she can hear it. It's under her chair. Pur-flop. Pur-flop. Louder still, like a spoon dropping on a shag pile carpet. Pur-flop. Flop.

'Lift me up. I have come to eat from your own plate.'

The girl scrapes her knife at the steak.

'Lift me up. I want to rest my chin on your hand.'

But the girl just sloshes wine into her glass and looks into the eyes of the man of her dreams.

That night, there it is again, on the stairs to her flat: Pur-flop. Pur-flop. Loudest yet, like gloved hands clapping. Pur-flop. Flop.

'Open the door. I want what you promised me. Open the door.'

And the girl gets out of bed and goes to the door, because the man of her dreams, her heart's desire, is stirring in his sleep, and what if he should wake up and hear the frog? What would he think? So she opens the door. The frog hops in. Pur-flop.

'Place me on your pillow,' the frog says, and the girl has no choice but to stick to the bargain. She puts the frog on her pillow, but she puts the pillow under the bed, and lies with her own head on the hard mattress.

And the next day, after the man of her dreams, her heart's desire, goes to work, she feeds the frog from her own breakfast bowl, puts him in her handbag and takes him to work. What else can she do? She puts the handbag on her desk but she doesn't let the frog out.

This goes on, and on. It stops her sleeping. It stops her working. The frog wants out of the bag, and on to the bed, and he wants and wants, louder and louder. What if the frog pur-flops out one night and wakes the man of her dreams? But her man, her heart's desire, is at her flat less and less. Perhaps it's the bags under her eyes, or the way she looks over her shoulder, or maybe she just can't hide her secret, no matter how far she pushes it under the bed. Pur-flop. Pur-flop. Soon enough, the man of her dreams tells her he's going to stop coming at all. She sits in her dressing gown for two days. The frog sits on the coffee table opposite her.

'Pick me up. It is time for me to eat from your own plate. Pick me up.'

The girl stares at him. Her mouth opens, as if to reveal something on her tongue.

'Get out, frog. I have lost my heart's desire. I don't owe you.'

'But it is you who lost him, not me. You must still feed me from your own plate, and lift me up to sleep on your pillow, and take me with you everywhere. All you have to do is love me and I will never leave you, nor betray you, nor break your heart. Isn't that your heart's desire?'

'Don't be ridiculous,' she shouts. 'How can I love a frog?' And she picks him up and throws him hard at the wall.

The frog hits the wall like a green beanbag, and slides down it to the floor. Then he gets up. And up. And up. He stands up straight, taller than her. He has long hands, thin legs, broad shoulders, green eyes and no hair on his chest at all. He smiles a wide smile.

So the frog, who is now a man, becomes her heart's desire. They live happily ever after, which means of course that sometimes they're happy and sometimes they're not. And one day, when they aren't so happy, she asks the man who was a frog, why her? What made him choose her, above all others? She waits for him to answer, waits for her heart's desire. She wants him to say; because only you could break the spell. Because you are special. Because you are unique. That's what she wants to hear.

'Because you happened to be passing,' he says, and so exacts his revenge.

Made For Each Other
Nichol Wilmor

Ned & Grace. Grace & Ned.

We are made for each other, thought Ned. What's more, Father will approve. Or would. If approval were in his nature.

'Remember, Edwin,' Father had told him. 'Most women are dangerously – yes – dangerously mad.'

It was the only thing Father had told him about women – or about anything else really – which is why Ned remembered it. He might have asked Father if Mother, too, had been 'dangerously mad'. But Father didn't talk about Mother. Ever.

Ned was certain he was safe with Grace. Grace wasn't mad. No. Grace was plainly, palpably, incontestably sane.

They had met in the brown surroundings of a coffee shop. ('The Bottomless Pot.') More accurately, they had found themselves there alone, the last people left on a Saturday night. Whether Grace had joined Ned or he had joined her, Ned couldn't now remember. Indeed most of the last month's memories were a muddle until the moment when he had found himself down on one awkward knee.

'Well, Edwin,' Grace had said, not unkindly, 'I shall have to see.'

And she had taken from her handbag a list of questions – very sensible questions – about love and marriage and money and property – which Ned had answered as truthfully as he could – 'Yes' / 'No' / 'No' / 'Yes' – while Grace ticked little boxes.

After the last question, Grace returned the list to her handbag.

'I will let you know, Edwin.'

Which she did. A day and a half later.

'Yes, Edwin,' she said. 'I will.'

'There's one thing,' Ned said. A single, timid misgiving. 'Do you think you could call me 'Ned'?'

'I shall try,' said Grace. 'Although 'Ned' is not how I see you.'

"Ned' is how I see myself,' thought Ned, although he said nothing.

*

Lilith & Henry. Henry & Lilith.

'They are made for each other!' said their friends.

Everyone who met them said the same and had done since the university dramatic society's autumn term audition. Arriving early, Lilith and Henry had seated themselves on two vacant thrones on a dais. (The summer term production had been The Taming of the Shrew.) This was the scene that revealed itself to the director when he scuttled in with his script and clipboard. Lilith and Henry. Elegant and languid. Effortless perfection. They were cast at once. Thenceforward, they were always cast. In every production. Neither of them, it must be admitted, was a prodigious talent but this wasn't the point. Lilith and Henry needed to be seen. More accurately, their friends needed to see them. Such a wonderful couple. She so golden, he so bronze, shimmering in a silver mist.

Later, when Lilith came to think about it, she couldn't remember when – or whether – she and Henry had made the decision to be together. It was as if it had been made for them. As if not to be together would have been to let everyone down. Lilith sometimes wondered if Henry felt the same.

For three enchanting years, social circles revolved around them. Hopes soared and tumbled. Loyalties were tested. Passions became enflamed. Love blazed and faded and blazed again. And at the still centre of everything were Lilith and Henry. Cool, calm, consummate. Surrounded by those who adored them. A consequence was that Lilith and Henry spent very little time together entirely alone – although those hours that they did spend in each other's company were perfectly pleasant.

Finals were finished. The wheel had started to slow. Soon the curtain would come down and the players would go their separate ways. An end was needed. A resolution was required. Or, if not 'required', wished for. Fervently. So fervently that disappointment would have been hard to bear.

'Will you, Lily?' Henry had said.

'Please, Henry. Never, never call me 'Lily'!'

The wedding – a cornucopia of lemon and cream – was staged in a Saxon parish church. Lilith's parents showed themselves as exquisite as their daughter, while Henry – unexpectedly – was found to be an orphan with a wealthy guardian who dispensed largesse from a rocky island he inhabited in the Highlands. It was, all their friends agreed, a charming way to end a most magical interlude.

*

Ned and Grace spent their honeymoon in Westward Ho! Whenever the rain stopped, they walked beside the sea and watched the grey Atlantic waves. Ned liked the sea but he had hoped for more. His dream had been to go to Venice. St Mark's Square, the Doge's Palace, the Teatro La Fenice. To lie with his love in a gondola under the Bridge of Sighs. But Grace had little time for dreams and the money they saved went towards the deposit on their flat in Muswell Hill.

*

Lilith and Henry spent their honeymoon in Verona. (Her mother's suggestion.) The hotel proposed the Menu Romeo & Giulietta. Henry chose Tris di Carpacci — Salmone, tonno e spada con citronette. Lilith chose Prosciutto crudo rustico con mozzarella di bufala. Lilith's was the wiser choice. Henry was ill all night. He was no better the next day. Nor the day after. When – three days later – he showed signs of recovery, Lilith left his bedside to explore the city alone. It was lovely, of course. But they were both happy to be home in the Parsons Green apartment that Henry's guardian had so thoughtfully provided for them.

*

Ned had warned Grace that Father might not attend their wedding so that, when he didn't, it was no surprise. But it was a shock to learn that – while they'd been in Westward Ho! – Father had remarried. And another shock when – a year later – his widow told them Father had died. Ned had always believed Father to be wealthy. He had the air of a wealthy man. But air, it seemed, was all he had. When the solicitor read out his will, it was plain that Father was penniless.

'No joy there then,' said Grace.

'No,' said Ned. 'None.'

*

Shortly after their return from Verona, Lilith and Henry learned that Henry's guardian had died. Lilith was on hand to offer comfort but Henry was stoical. Finding himself unexpectedly rich, Henry's plans to seek glittering employment seemed suddenly redundant. No matter. He adapted to leisure readily and devoted his time to jazz. Lilith didn't like jazz. She detested its rasp and rattle. But couples can't share everything, she reasoned, and she had her little job in the art gallery to occupy her.

*

An aside. (There will be others.) Marriage is a tricky business. Or can be, for a year or two, while you find out who it is you've married. Sex may sometimes smooth the path. Although sex can be tricky, too.

*

Grace knew about sex and marriage. She had read up on the subject and highlighted and underlined several passages. Her regime was regular. On Thursday nights and – for variety – on Sunday mornings. There were seldom any hiccups. It was,

Grace thought, satisfactory and quite sufficient. Tender gestures at other times led Ned nowhere. With brisk efficiency Grace removed his hand from below her breast; soft music would be turned off sharply; red roses were taken straight to the sink where their tender stalks were trimmed with sharp kitchen scissors. Was it ungrateful to want more? Ned wondered. But more, he couldn't deny, was what he wanted. Although more of what he wasn't sure.

*

Before Henry, sex for Lilith had been something of a trial. She had nothing against it. Not a thing. But so much of her early youth had been spent defending herself against encroaching hands, busy tongues and pressing flesh that it had quite exhausted her. Henry was therefore a relief. He was tender, delicate, considerate. Almost too considerate. Lilith had imagined – she didn't know why – that marriage would change things. It didn't. Theirs wasn't exactly a sexual desert but the image of a neglected allotment often sprang to mind. Once, when, delicately, she had raised the topic – as one would with a stranger – Henry replied, 'I'm afraid sex doesn't do much for me.' And added, 'I hope that's all right?' Lilith nodded – as one does with strangers – but she was almost certain that it wasn't.

*

Marco & Flo.

No, no, no. It won't work. No. So it was said – in English and Italian – by their friends and relations. (In Italian to their faces; in English behind their backs.) Were they right?

There isn't time to tell you how Marco and Flo met at Victoria Station. (He was an hour and a quarter early for a train to Hastings while she should have been at Charing Cross.) Nor how Marco – tall and correct – harboured a desire to be English, while Flo – plump and chaotic – yearned to be extravagantly Italian. Absurd, of course. As absurd as falling in love. Particularly as Marco's English was limited and Flo's Italian was flawed.

(Although, it may be remarked, Marco and Flo were fluent in that language where sounds are more eloquent than words.) Nor is there time to tell you about their wedding at the Euston Road Registry Office, attended only by Uncle Hugo who, as a young man, had fallen in love with an Italian beauty in Rimini, been warned by his family that – should he marry her – he could expect to inherit nothing, and had, with a breaking heart, taken a train back to England and lived thereafter a bone-dry bachelor's life in Georgian Bath. Uncle Hugo had always been fond of Flo, took a liking to Marco and happily provided the money they required to open the Ponte Vecchio, a modest eatery in Camden's Little Italy. No, there's no time to tell you this. Besides Flo and Marco and Uncle Hugo are secondary characters and we must return to our principals.

*

Time passed.

'Life is passing,' thought Ned in Muswell Hill, in the dark days of early February.

'Like muddy bubbles in a sluggish stream,' thought Lilith in Parsons Green.

'I must do something,' Ned told himself, sternly.

'But what?' Lilith asked herself, mournfully.

*

'I have booked a table for Valentine's Night,' Ned told Grace.

'I have booked a table for Valentine's Night,' Lilith told Henry.

'Nowhere expensive, I hope,' said Grace.

'Oh,' said Henry.

*

It is no coincidence that both Ned and Lilith booked tables at the Ponte Vecchio; it is only because they did that they appear in this story at all. Nor is it a coincidence that their tables were next to each other; they were the only tables available. (The year before two other couples had booked the same tables at the back of the restaurant under the antique wine rack. During the course of the evening they had struck up a conversation and pushed their two tables together. The friendship that started that night blossomed through the year. In January they booked the same tables – although, as it happened, now they were two different couples. Later, they'd had second thoughts. It might, they felt, be awkward. And they cancelled their bookings. Which is why both tables were available when – within minutes of each other – first Ned and then Lilith telephoned the Ponte Vecchio.) It is, however, a coincidence that on the thirteenth of February two couples – one in Muswell Hill, the other in Parsons Green – were listening to Tosca. (Although they were listening to different recordings.) It is the kind of coincidence that is frowned upon in fiction but allowable in fact. You are therefore free to frown but this is what happened.

*

Grace didn't dislike opera especially. It was music she didn't care for. Why then was she sitting there with Ned? She really couldn't say.

Henry hoped Lilith would leave the room. Or fall asleep. Or something. It was frustrating when she didn't. He was aching to play Thelonius Monk.

At last it was over.

Tosca had jumped from the ramparts and fallen to her death.

Grace looked up from her crossword.

Henry fidgeted on the sofa.

Ned and Lilith sat in their silences, trying to decipher what they were feeling.

> *Entrava ella fragrante,*
> *mi cadea fra la braccia.*
> She entered, fragrant,
> And fell into my arms.

(Ned read in the notes.)

L'ora è fuggita, e muoio disperato!
E non ho amato mai tanto la vita!

The moment has flown and I die in despair!

Never have I loved life so much.

(Lilith translated; she had studied Italian in Perugia.)

Yearning is so difficult to describe. A humming. A thrubbing. A sharp emptiness. A dull agony. The tick-tick-tick of a wall-clock. The sigh of a slowly spinning globe.

'I hold the key to something,' thought Ned. 'Something special, something mystical, something magical. But what – what – will it open?'

'I am trapped, ensnared, enchained,' thought Lilith. 'I must find my release. But who – who – will release me?'

*

Grace broke the silence.

'What I can never understand in opera, Edwin, is why, when characters have something to say, they feel the need to sing it?'

Henry couldn't bear it any longer.

'My problem with opera, Lily,' he said, 'is that it is so emotional.'

*

Ned made his decision that night.

And Lilith made hers.

The next morning they both caught trains. Ned travelled from St Pancras and Lilith from Waterloo. I can't tell you where they went because they have left the story. But neither of them remembered to cancel their bookings at the Ponte Vecchio.

*

The Ponte Vecchio is always fully-booked on Valentine's Night and Marco is mildly irritated to find that the two tables under the antique wine rack have remained unoccupied. But, he decides, he won't think about this until the morning.

The last diners have left and Flo is locking the door. Marco takes down the bottle of Barolo that he has set aside. Together they go into the kitchen. Flo lights a candle and Marco pours the wine. They hold up their glasses and look into each other's eyes. They smile. There is no hurry. And no need to speak. When the bottle is empty, Marco will blow out the candle and take Flo's hand. It would be indelicate to follow them up the stairs. Or to say any more.

Truth, Music, and NikkiSexKitten
Jason Jackson

NikkiSexKitten's new message flashes up on screen. She wants to know who my teenage fantasy was.

So I post back. Blondie, I say. The Divine Debbie. The way she looked at the camera. Her legs. Her lips. This is what I type, grinning. I sip the last of my beer, and I stare at the screen.

NikkiSexKitten posts back quickly. I look like Debbie Harry, she says. Blonde hair. Red lips. Short, short skirts.

I stand up, run to the fridge, crack open another beer, and I'm back in front of the screen, typing. What are you wearing now? I type.

What do you want me to be wearing?

And okay, it's a cliché, and okay, I know she's lying, and she's probably fourteen stone and bald, but it's February 14th, nearly midnight, and her lies are all I've got.

I type quickly. You remember the Heart of Glass video, I say, the one where she's wearing an off the shoulder grey-green chiffon dress, black tights, black stilettos? That's what I want you to be wearing.

I wait.

But she doesn't post back.

Maybe she never saw the video.

So I log off. I go to bed. I switch on cable and flick through the music channels, vaguely hoping for Heart of Glass, or Union City Blue, or something, just to relive those teenage years, but I don't find anything at all, and then it's Monday, and I'm at work, and I'm losing my job.

'But Mr Kenfield,' I say. 'Reg,' I say.

He pauses, sitting there behind his desk, with his cooler-than-you glasses, his severe hair, his fucking aftershave-aura, and he waits. He actually waits for what I have to say. But there's just silence. The truth is, of course, that I have nothing whatsoever to say. Unless I had the balls to say, yes, Reggie-baby, I've been surfing the net during work-time, I frequent chat-rooms where I interact with the likes of ZoeStarFucker, KellyYesPlease and of course NikkiSexKitten, and I do all this on your time, Reggie, because I have the modern-day curse of a job that is beneath my intellectual ability coupled with a lack of a life-partner to minister to my every sexual proclivity. Yes, Reggie, I am sad, lonely, bored, horny, and severely lacking any sense of direction or fulfilment. And while doing all of this, Reggie, I was fully aware that I'd be caught. And you know what? It didn't stop me. And do you know why? Because I care very little for your opinion of me as a person, and I care less about the fucking job. So. Sack me. And by the way, your hair's shit.

That's what I'd say if I had the balls.

What I actually say is, 'Would sorry make a difference?'

Of course, sorry doesn't make the slightest difference, and by twelve-thirty I'm an unemployed man eating a stringy pizza out of a cardboard box while sat on a bench in the park, waiting for it to rain. When it starts, I don't move. There is something noble about eating pizza in the rain. It singles you out from your fellow man, the hordes running from the park for shelter in the nearby shops, laughing, holding hands, thinking that far from being an inconvenience the rain actually adds to their lunchtime park experience, a little romantic interlude to be mentioned over dinner that night, hey darling, wasn't it just nuts when we were in the park today and it started to rain and we had to run into Borders and that car nearly hit you and just think, if it hadn't started to rain we would never have bought this CD, and who's it by again, oh yeah, that woman who we saw on television last night, and hasn't she got just a great voice?

I take another bite of pizza, and I just sit there watching

the ducks. I don't think about work. I don't think about going home. I don't think about how the fuck I'm going to pay the rent next week. What I think about is NikkiSexKitten, or not so much her – I have no idea who she is above a cute little avatar of a cartoon fairy with little wings and yellow hair – but about what we were posting about last night. Blondie. And, suddenly, I have a Nick-Hornby-in-High-Fidelity moment. I decide that what I really need in my life is a female singer. Preferably a singer-songwriter. A slightly kooky, fully intellectual, talented, famous-ish but not too famous, preferably heavily-eyelinered and waif-like, guitar-playing girl. Or woman. In fact, a girl-woman would be just about ideal. I want eye contact, a conversation – ideally over coffee, or alcohol – an invite to her next gig, then – backstage – some hand-holding and flirting, kisses, first without, then with, tongues, then back to her attic (it doesn't have to be an attic, but it's a fantasy), not into bed (come on, imagination) but out onto a balcony (yes) in the rain (yes, yes) with a bottle of wine – no, fuck that, vodka – where we make love under a star-less sky, and afterwards I hang off the balcony by one hand and declare that I am staying exactly where I am until she writes a song about me, which she does, right there on the balcony with her beat-up twelve-string, and she sings it, not to me but to the heavens and the angels, and when she finishes I pull myself back onto the balcony and we fall into a tight embrace, the guitar and the rain and the song and the vodka forgotten, because all there is in the world is the two of us, forever, lovers together, and we'll never, ever have to lie to each other…

I throw the pizza box at the ducks, then I walk to the tube.

Inside the station, down in the tunnels, there's a busker. I hear her before I see her, and I'm thinking that I know the song but I can't place it. There's a nice sound to the guitar because of the acoustics, her voice is strong, and I turn the corner just as she gets to a line I recognise so I mouth the words as she sings them: *in the flesh.*

It's probably my least favourite song by Blondie, but the way she's doing it, kind of up-tempo, almost rockabilly in style, gives it a life, a bounce that the original never had, and she's even doing a little jig to go with it. She's as tall as me at least, and her hair's cut short, but there's hardly anything of her. She's wearing a big black vest, leggings that bag out at the knees and boots, really, really big boots. Her arms are skinny, and the taut, thin muscles stand out as she plays, beating, pulling, prodding at the guitar. It's not pretty, and she's hardly the girl-woman of my park daydream, but I stop about twenty yards from her and I watch.

She finishes the song, looks down at her guitar case, fiddles with the neck of her guitar, and looks around. Then she's into another song, something I don't recognise, something slower, and sad. I stay exactly where I am, and I stare at her. I'm looking at a woman, a real woman, a singer, a guitar player, and she's singing these words that are echoing off the walls of a tunnel that I walk through most days of my life, and I realise how long it is since I talked to someone, not just work-drones who I moan at and who moan back at me every fucking day, and not NikkiSexKitten and all the rest who are just words on a screen in my darkened room, but someone, a real someone, someone who might listen to me, who might actually let me tell the truth for a change. I realise how long it is since I made a sound that mattered, and as I watch the people walk past her, no one even looks at her, and no one puts any money in her case, and yet there she is, singing this beautiful song and I'm suddenly convinced that it's her own song, that she's sick of doing covers so she's doing her own stuff, words that she wrote, that she wants people to hear, her truth, and fuck it if they don't listen, or no one gives her any money, because the song is the thing, the words are the thing, and here she is, singing them, and I'm watching them bounce off the tunnel walls and the people around her, and I'm smiling.

I get a pen from my pocket and pull out the insert in my

fag packet. I rest on the wall behind me, and as she sings about a sky, a clear sky, I write the words *thank you* on the paper. I start to walk towards her, and I know that I won't look at her, that it's not about her now, it's about me, and I can daydream in the park as much as I like about lovers on balconies and vodka kisses, but in the end what it comes down to – this fucking life – is standing in the painful gaze of the world and singing your truth into its ugly and dispassionate face.

As I pass the girl I drop the note into her case, and I walk down towards the tube, listening as the music disappears, knowing exactly where I'm going.

Three stops away from this station is a shop that sells guitars.

Ringtone
Harry Whitehead

Johnny squats in a doorway, crying like he's teething. Snot flows salty down his lips. It drips onto his hands.

He's spent the evening at The Queen and Artichoke in Camden with Tall Tom the director, hatching plans to shoot a short film together.

In the pub, Johnny's mobile goes. He's got a ringtone he made up himself: 'Johnny…Hey, Johnny. Johnny. Johnny! JOHNNY…OI JOHNNY! JOOHHNNNY!' On the phone, it's Chloe, his girlfriend. She wants to know when he's planning on getting home. Should she cook dinner? Johnny say's he'll be back at closing time. She's cool. Never gets on his case.

Tall Tom likes the ringtone. Maybe they could use it in the short film. Johnny's not sure where, but he nods anyway, bleary with Stella and scotch.

Later, at home, Johnny leans on the bathroom door while Chloe soaks.

'We got a great idea for a short,' he says. 'It's about this girl with huge hands who's training a seagull to do loop the loops. It'd be kind of dark and macro focus in the details. You know… avant garde.' He trails off.

'Super,' says Chloe absently, scrubbing her shoulders with an expensive sponge from Madagascar. 'You know,' she says, 'I've been thinking. The front room: it's all a bit samey, isn't it? I reckon we should paint the wall behind the TV something bright. Like a brilliant yellow.'

Johnny stares in at her, silent. Then, as she's drying off, he rails. 'You're nowhere fucking near me, are you? You don't get me at all…what it takes to make things happen in my world!'

She looks at him blankly through wet, black wisps of hair. Chloe runs a nightclub. Johnny stands there feeling like a man in jeans and trainers.

'Fuck the yellow wall.' There's a half-full wine glass on the coffee table. He picks it up and throws it at the wall above the TV. 'How about red? That'd be nice.' There are more glasses and plates on the dining table. He throws them at the wall as well. 'Fucking ripple effect?' Johnny's such a funny, funny guy. He loathes himself even as he does it.

So he kicks the sofa hard enough for it to jump into the air. He nearly breaks his foot. Then he grabs the car keys and limps out, leaving her naked and silent in the lounge, still holding the wet towel in her hand. He's can't find the car and, within a minute or so, he's forgotten the keys are in his pocket anyway.

He falls into a doorway and wails like a lost cat. The mucus gurgles in his throat. He gasps and he chokes and he moans, and nothing comes through the liquor to make it any easier to bear. Whatever it might be.

'Darling, you alright?' It's a shock through the violence of his misery. Johnny won't look up. Not into another person's eyes. He mutters a few incomprehensible words and hopes the do-gooder will just fuck off. Or he hopes they'll pick him up and make it all better. Snot runs off the back of his hand, making a tightrope line between shirt-cuff and knee. He moans again, a sound of hard pain. A warning or an entreaty.

'Come on.' The figure kneels down. He sees boots and the wave of a skirt revealing bare knees. Who is this? He squints through the refraction of his streetlight tears, trying to focus, sobs still bubbling out of him.

A teenage girl with a sharp face and a concerned mouth, her hair spiky with a streak of some colour he can't make out in the sodium glow. She tries to put her arms round him. He mumbles her off, but he doesn't mean it.

'What's up?' she says. 'Eh? Had some kind of row with

your girlfriend?'

' 'Muh-right.' Johnny's words gargle through the spittle in his throat.

'If you get up, you can talk to me better, can't you?' She pulls at him and he levers forward a bit. 'Up you get, darling.' Johnny allows himself to be hauled up. He leans back against the door for a moment. 'You want to tell me what's going on, then?'

'I can't…it's just…' his chest heaves. 'Short…seagull…' He breathes for a bit. 'A lot of shit come down all at once, is all.' She's caught enough of his attention to hold him. She's cute, he thinks; she's cute, isn't she?

'You want to come with me? I only live round the corner. I'll make us a cup of tea and you can calm down a bit.' He whispers a few protests, but now he's somewhere between the misery of his home life predicament – whatever that is – and some low-intensity guilt at talking to this girl fifty yards from the flat he shares with Chloe: a sweet-feeling guilt, sugared with dawning sexual possibility.

The girl takes his arm, ignoring his half-hearted objections. He leans into her and finds himself resting his head on her shoulder. They walk, and, as they walk, she runs her fingers lightly across his arse, quickly but with just enough intent for him to know there's no mistake.

He's coming round again now alright. They stop then and, as he stands on his own and wipes at his face with the back of his sleeve, he looks at her properly. She must be, what, twenty? She's sexy, yes, the short hair giving a boyish frame to a cutesy face. There's just a hint of something about her though. What is it? A hardness somewhere? Something narrow in the line of her smile.

She meets his gaze. 'Bit better now?' She moves in closer, still looking him right in the eye. Johnny goes to kiss her and she doesn't push him away. He licks at her mouth, some kind of anger – call it revenge – adding to the lust, making him nearly lose his balance. He falls against her and her hands scrabble all over him. They move up his back inside his coat and one hand plays across his cock. He gropes at her breasts and her arse.

This goes on a moment longer and then she pushes him backwards, friendly but to the point. 'Oi, easy tiger!' Johnny staggers back a bit, dizzy for a moment.

And then the curtains pull back and he can see again through the windows of his street-savvy. He peers more closely at her.

'So where exactly are we going, then?' he says.

'My gaff's just down the road.' She sounds different now, tighter, her lips thin. 'Where d'you live anyway?' she says.

He looks around him, up and down the street, getting his bearings. About twenty yards away, there's a pedestrian passageway leading between the Victorian terraced houses to the next road. A man stands, half in shadow, watching them.

Of course he does.

'I'm just back here,' Johnny says. 'You know what, though, I feel a lot better. I reckon I might just go home now.'

'Alright. Good.' She turns away. As she does so, his mobile phone rings. 'Johnny…Hey, Johnny. Johnny. Johnny! JOHNNY…OI JOHNNY! JOOHHNNNY!'

The thing is, it's coming from her pocket.

She looks at him, afraid.

He laughs. He laughs on and on until he chokes and coughs. He can see she doesn't know what to do. It looks like she wants to run off, but she doesn't get it. It just makes him laugh all the more. He's laughing like he's nuts, like he's dangerous. He knows that's how it seems, and it makes him laugh even more – loving the power of it over her.

After some moments, his hysterics retreat enough for him to speak.

'Just give me back my phone,' he digs around in his pockets. 'And my wallet, alright?' He moves towards her. They are standing right in the middle of the empty street.

'What the fuck you doing to her?' The man emerges now into the streetlight. Johnny just starts laughing again. It stops pimp-man, bad-arse, whoever-the-fuck-he-is, in his tracks as well.

'Mate, I don't care,' says Johnny. 'I really don't. But your girl's nicked my phone and my wallet, and it's just gone off in her pocket. It's fucking genius.' She backs away now down the road. 'I just want my wallet and my phone back.'

Johnny meets the man face on. He's thin with a sharp scar running from the outside of his eye to the front of his chin. It stands out pale against the darker skin of his face. He's young, which, even pissed as he is, Johnny knows is bad news. But the guy doesn't get the laughing thing either.

'Look,' Johnny says to the girl, 'just take whatever cash is in the wallet and give it back to me with my phone, alright? I'm not gonna do anything. Honest. You cheered me up. It's worth it.' She's still backing away. 'I'm not gonna do anything!'

She looks in the wallet and pulls some notes out. She pulls the phone from her coat pocket. She holds it and the wallet out towards Johnny, just as it makes the sound to say there's a message – woodleydoodleydoo. That sets Johnny off again. Even she almost smiles.

Johnny watches the man more than he watches her now, as he steps forward and takes his things back. The man's still not sure. Maybe he thought she had a score, but now that she's a thief he doesn't know what to do?

'Take it easy, sweetie.' Johnny turns around and walks away up the road, leaving the two still standing in the sodium-lit silence. He doesn't walk too fast, but he's not hanging around either. He listens to see if their footsteps follow him, feeling crystal clear now. Round the first corner and he stops for a moment, leaning against a wooden fence. He looks at his mobile. The call was from Chloe.

Five minutes later, having ducked and turned to throw

off any scent trails, he stands outside his front door. He sees the lights are off. Chloe seems to have gone to bed. He's got a tale to tell, though it's not the sort of thing she's going to want to hear, is it?

Still, it'd make a great short film. He squints at the screen on his mobile, scrolling for Tall Tom's number. A lot cheaper than teaching a fucking seagull to do loop the loops.

The Runner
Alan McCormick

Last night you had been drunk, but not legless. You had checked your run in a camera shop window along the Strand. You were surprised by the uniformity of your stride; even after the altercation.

You had been at the work Christmas party. You had used alcohol to free up your self-expression. You liked yourself when you drank; you were funny. You had told jokes, some unusual, and had chatted up one of the secretaries from litigation – the one you've always liked, the one who looks up and smiles when she types, the one who last night told you she had a boyfriend. She had repeated this seven times, only because you kept saying, 'have I died and gone up to heaven, because I see an angel standing before me?'

By the third time she replied she was no longer smiling, and by the seventh she was crying. You were shocked by this reaction and took yourself to the bar for a few vodkas where you shouted that she'd led you on and that women weren't angels, they were rat-like witches with broomsticks for tails. That was when the security man – he had the acme smell of Brut and wore the uniform of a traffic warden – tapped you on the shoulder.

Was that the altercation? You can't be sure, but blood from your fingers has left a tell-tale imprint on your sheets this morning. Had you smashed a bottle? You can't remember but you do remember there was blood on the soles of your feet when you got in to your flat.

You were running out of the hotel when you saw your boss say something, and for some reason, maybe the zeitgeist of footballers spitting at each other, you spat at him. You missed but it hit his father, the septuagenarian Life-President, and he had just stood there amazed. You were chased and your chest hurt, but your legs, your regular legs kept pumping.

As you ran into the night you thought about the 1500 metres and your boyhood hero, Steve Ovett, infinitely preferable and sexier than that squirt Coe. As you imagined Steve Cram in chase you found yourself running down an alleyway. At the end of it, you bumped into a car: a police car.

A young policeman spoke polite young policeman lines:

'You're in a hurry, sir. Is everything okay?'

You started jogging on the spot. 'I'm perfectly fine, officer, I'm practising for the Olympics.'

That was the folly of drink speaking and you knew it as soon as you'd said it.

'Very good, sir, but why don't you calm down and stand still for a moment?'

'I need to get home,' you whined.

'What's the hurry, sir?'

'No hurry.'

'You appear to be upset,' he said.

'I'm happy as Larry,' you said, still pumping the spot.

You wanted him to say, 'who's Larry?', but he didn't, he just kept on:

'Has something or someone upset you?'

Stalling was proving an irrelevance and so you took up the pistol start and ran. The other policeman emerged from the shadows and tripped you up. You went sprawling, saved your face with your hands, cut your fingers in the process.

The polite policeman helped you up. The tripper police-man, larger and scarier than the other, took up the baton; he had a loud squeaky voice like he'd sucked up a blast of helium: 'Now stand still and bloody answer.'

Good cop, bad cop. Nice cop, squeaky cop. You said the former.

'No, both bad cops. Now, what's your name?' asked Squeaky.

'Steve Cram,' you replied.

'The runner?' said Nice, taking back the baton.

'Ovett, I mean.'

They stared at you.

'I have a race to get to.'

Nice then pointed out that you had a name badge on the left lapel of your jacket.

'It's not my name.'

'Then that's not your jacket, is it, sir?'

'No, it is my jacket; there was just a mix up with name badges.'

'Who got yours: Sebastian Coe?' asked Squeaky.

'Shall we take it that your name is Paul McMasters, sir,' said Nice reading from your badge.

'If you like.'

'Otherwise,' Squeaky slipped in, 'otherwise we could be asking you how you got to be wearing Mister Coe's jacket.'

You were confused. They were smiling. A short moment passed without anything being said.

'Do you realise it's an offence to impersonate someone else?' they said together like a comedy duo. Your head was full of Mike Yarwood though. Squeaky continued: 'and that it's an offence to give false information to the police.'

'And that anything you say from now on will be noted down in evidence and could be used should a criminal prosecution arise from any of your answers to our questions,' said Nice, but no longer that nice.

'I'm a solicitor,' you said.

'Not a runner?' they said.

'I'm a solicitor, I'm a solicitor,' you repeated.

They took your name and address and you told them that you had got drunk and had disgraced yourself at the work Christmas party. You told them that you were still drunk and that you were 'very, very sorry'. They seemed to like this; valued your candour and sense of remorse. They warned you about your future conduct and cautioned you that they would keep a record of the conversation for the duration of the night in case your details tallied with any disturbance or incident later. After that they would lose the paperwork.

Your legal brain liked that term 'lose the paperwork' – short circuiting, a camaraderie transaction of the law amongst professionals; not making it up, just saving time. You thanked them and they offered to drop you at a night bus stop.

'No. no,' you said. 'I need to get some air, Dave. You understand?'

Dave, the nice one understood, and Bruce, the other one grinned and gave you the thumbs up.

'Run along now, Paul,' they said, and you did.

So you had got to know their names, you must have been speaking to them for ages. So many gaps to fill: what exactly did you say and do to make them like you? You didn't know but you wish you hadn't said you were a solicitor; you're a legal assistant. They can check on things like that and then where would you be? You weren't sure of the answer to this but you knew you were running down a street towards the night buses in Trafalgar Square, where you convinced yourself that it was a busy night and that they weren't going to be bothered to check over small details.

Revellers were everywhere and they all seemed drunk, alcohol fumes igniting the sky and the smell of perfume and male deodorant rubbing against you as people toppled into you. Brute pheromones and sweaty violence emanating off the packs of bouncers lurking in bomber jackets outside their clubs – splash it all over and dig you in the ribs down an alleyway – you steered a wide berth and thought they looked like devil dogs, Rottweilers like in Omen, pawing the sky and baring their teeth. One grinned at you and pointed and you gave him a V sign and upped your running pace to get away.

Girls in miniskirts and angry ice-pick heels formed into Conga lines that snaked in and out of your path. One pulled your tie and you wavered for a moment before breaking free. She called you Darren and said she'd snogged you in Cinderella's. Then when she saw your face, she said 'sorry mate' and the other girls laughed, their naughty elf Christmas hats and tinsel jewellery shaking, shrill screams scraping up the buildings and into the night.

You pulled off your jacket and tie and put them in a bin. There was a reason beyond the heat of running; something to do with not being recognised. Might have been easier to just lose the badge, but soon your trousers were gone too, and so you knew it was time you got on the bus. You found one of those single disabled seats on the ground floor facing the door. The bus was full. Somehow you kept hold of your travel card and your mobile phone: 'I'm not that drunk' you kept saying to yourself.

You had told Dave and Bruce that you'd be walking home. And there you were, undressed on a bus. Technically that was a lie, another one. But then Crystal Palace was a long way to walk so they'd have known you were lying anyway. 'Hardly credible at this time of night,' you thought you remembered Bruce squeaking.

'Shut the fuck up,' you said.

You said it out loud and so everyone on the bus stared at you.

Then you looked away and pressed your face against the window. Soon you were passing the party hotel again. You wiped away the condensation from the glass. There was an ambulance and a police car; blue lights revolving at different levels, Dave and Bruce getting out of their car.

'Fascists,' you whispered against the glass, leaving the imprint of your kiss.

An hour later when the bus rolled into the garage, the fluorescent lights inside flashed and the driver jabbed you on the shoulder.

'Fuck off, Paul,' he said.

He knew your name because during the journey you had kept shouting your name out, saying you were Paul Ovett, the little known brother of Steve.

You were in Crystal Palace now. Your flat was left at the top of the high street, but you went the other way. You found the stadium in the park. The air smelled sweet up there and the city blinked below like a million cats' eyes. The all-weather track had a fine orange powdery surface that scratched the soles of your feet. Barefoot, in boxers and vest, you were running like Zola Budd. Nearly four times round the track, 1500 metres, in less than five minutes. Not Olympic, but pretty good considering. You punched the black night air in victory as you crossed the line.

On the run home your mobile rang. It was John from accounts.

'What happened to you, matey? We were worried about you, running off like a nutter. Went outside and looked for you and everything.'

'Did you find me?' you asked.

'Uh? Anyway, you missed a cracking night. Old Mister Bert had a heart attack and everything.'

You remembered your spit.

'Did they see who did it?' you asked.

'You're toast, mate.'

You thought about the phrase.

'Anyway, I've left with Sheila, the little typist from litigation. She's just popped into a garage for the necessaries. Hope you don't mind.'

The phone revolved in the night sky, a small tinny 'sorry mate' gasping out before it landed on the street in pieces.

It is morning. The alarm clock has been silenced; you will not be going into work.

'Serve them right for having a party on a Thursday night,' you tell yourself.

You see your feet sticking out of the duvet, fine orange dust between your toes. You notice the blood. You look around your room, your posters of runners – Steve Ovett, of course, with pride of place over the mantelpiece, above the line of your junior cups and pennants.

Must keep hydrated; you go to the kitchen and fill up a pint glass with water. You notice the cuts on your fingers. Your heart turns and you feel sick. The only cure you know is to run. In your bedroom you open your wardrobe to look at yourself in the full-length mirror. You are naked, running on the spot, and you will stay there and run until all the poison leaks out.

Telling It Like It Is
James Smyth

'A hippo,' says Trev, sinking his Stella. 'Definitely. Slow moving, innit?'

'Fuck off,' I say, sinking mine. 'Have you seen the teeth on it? It'd rip your head off.'

We're drinking in the Bull's Head, and trying to decide what animals we could do over in a fight. I thought I was pushing it with the Shire horse, but there's no fucking way I'm having a hippo. Thing is, Trev fancies himself as a hard nut, with his gold chains and his signet rings. But I'd like to see him in a rumble with a fucking hippo. Not a chance, mate. Not a chance.

'You saying I couldn't take a hippo?' he says through a mouthful of pork scratchings, signalling to the bar for two more pints. 'It's just like a bigger version of a pig, innit? And we've already established that I could take out a pig with me hands behind me back.'

'I'm not saying you couldn't take out a pig, mate,' I say. The pints have arrived, and I down mine in one. 'I'm just saying that a hippo is a whole different proposition. Fucking massive, they are. Seen 'em on telly.'

Trev ruminates on this for a moment, spitting pork scratchings down his Chelsea top.

'Still reckon I could have it,' he says eventually. He has his eyes closed and his brow is furrowed, and I know he's imagining the scenario.

'You couldn't, mate,' I say reasonably.

'Well what the fuck do you know? When was the last time you were in a ruck?' Trev's piggy eyes are suddenly ablaze with anger. He always gets like this around about the eight-pint mark.

'Come on now, mate,' I say, holding up my hands. 'I glassed that cunt down at the Butcher's Arms last week, remember?'

For a second Trev looks like he's about to turn the table over, but at the last moment he seems to think better of it. He sits back.

'Yeah, I s'pose,' he admits sulkily. 'Are we moving onto chasers yet, or what?'

I go to the bogs while Trev gets the drinks in. There's a speccy little geezer stood next to me at the pisser, and for a second I think about pushing him into the trough, just for a laugh, but in the end I can't be arsed. I'm still thinking about the hippo. And the more I think about it, the more I start to get angry. I mean, I'm not saying Trev can't be a bit handy. He's not barred from ninety percent of the local pubs for nothing. And I've seen him take on blokes twice his size and come out smiling. But a fucking hippo? Who the fuck does he think he is?

I notice the speccy geezer is looking at me strangely, and realise that I must have been muttering about hippos under my breath. I give him the look.

'Problem, mate?' I say. He steps back, shaking his head. He's still got his knob out – fair size for a little bloke, to be honest – and he's pissing on his shoes. I put a heavy hand on his shoulder.

'Do you know how big a hippo is?' I say, lowering my head towards his.

'How big –?' Speccy looks just about ready to shit himself.

'They're fucking massive,' I say. 'Seen 'em on the telly. Trev doesn't know what the fuck he's talking about.'

I leave him to dry off his shoes, and go back to the bar. Trev is sitting there with two double whiskies.

'Got any nuggets?' he says. 'Fruitie looks like it wants to pay out.'

I hold up a hand.

'Look, mate,' I say. 'You know I totally respect you, yeah?

96

As a geezer?' Trev nods slowly. 'And as a mate. And I don't want us to fall out, right? '

I can see the muscles under Trev's Chelsea shirt starting to bunch, in readiness.

'Yeah ...' he says, slowly.

'And I know that you're one of the hardest blokes in Essex, yeah? And there's nobody I'd rather have backing me up if it all kicks off.'

'Yeee-ah,' says Trev.

'But,' I say, 'I've got to tell you something, mate. And I've been thinking about this a lot. And I wouldn't say this unless I'd properly thought it through, yeah?'

Trev is almost on his feet now. He knows something's up. I soldier on.

'And the fact is ...' I point a finger into his fat, pink face, and emphasise every word, for effect. 'You. Could. Not. Stove. In. A. Hippo.'

There is a second, where what I've just put out there sort of hangs in the air between us. For a minute, I think that this might all end all right. Then Trev picks up his whisky, drains it in one, and looks me straight in the eye.

'Listen, cunt,' he says, his voice like gravel. 'Nobody, and I mean nobody, tells me that I can't stove in a hippo. Now. Do you want to take that back?'

Trev's in full battle stance now, and I've got to admit, he is pretty tasty in a ruck. I think for a second that maybe I should back down, maybe I should say whatever he wants to hear, and we can go back to our drinks and the night might not end in bloodshed and broken fingers and another fucking night in casualty.

But then I think: a hippo? A fucking hippo? I open my mouth, and the words seem to come from nowhere:

'Mate,' I hear myself say, 'The only hippo you could beat in a fight, would be ... a gay hippo.'

A pause, while the bombshell drops. And then we're off. Trev barrels towards me, fists flying. I try to dodge out of the way, but he's fucking quick for a fat bastard, and before I know it he's on top of me, and I can smell the sweat and the lager on his breath. He's trying to get some body blows in, and I lower my arms to protect my ribs. I hear the familiar sound of breaking glass.

'Fucking ... hippos ...' grunts Trev, channelling his rage as he rolls about on top of me, limbs spasticking around.

'You're a ... fucking hippo,' I grunt back, trying to get him in a headlock, but finding that his neck's too thick for me to get my arm around.

'Just a big fucking pig,' growls Trev, launching his knee towards my groin.

'Massive teeth,' I say, reeling back from a head butt, the taste of blood in my mouth. 'Seen 'em on the fucking ...'

'HIPPOS!' roars Trev, and from the corner of my eye I see his gold-spangled fist come flying towards me. I don't even have time to flinch. He connects, I feel the crunch and the spurt of blood, and then it all goes dark.

*

I wake up in the back of an ambulance. With my tongue, I establish that I've lost at least two teeth. There's a nurse – a pretty fit one – sat beside me, looking disapproving.

'Awake, now, are we?' she says. I try to move my arm, but it won't budge. It feels solid, like a block of wood.

'Yeah,' I mutter. 'What's the damage?'

'It's not good,' she says. 'That friend of yours really went to town. He's with the police now.'

The more I think about it, the more I realise how many parts of my body I can't feel. Maybe this isn't just another Saturday night, I think. Maybe this is fucking serious.

'I can't feel my legs,' I mumble weakly.

The nurse purses her lips and shakes her head.

'Don't expect any sympathy from me,' she says. 'You know how much time I spend picking up after people like you?' I can see in her eyes that she's properly pissed off. 'I don't know,' she says, 'do you actually enjoy fighting? Is it fun? Does it not occur to you that it might be more pleasant just to have a conversation?'

I can taste blood on my tongue when I speak. What's left of my tongue.

'We were ... we were having a conversation,' I say.

'Oh really?' the nurse sneers. 'What, about whether some fucking football team is better than some other fucking football team?'

I'm suddenly aware of a piercing pain in my spine.

'No,' I say. 'It was about ... well, it was mostly about ...' the nurse raises an eyebrow, expectantly. 'Oh for fuck's sake,' I say, 'it doesn't matter now.'

*

The next morning it's on the news. I'm watching it on the telly in the hospital, dosed up on morphine and still in a lot of fucking pain. The doctors haven't given me the full story yet, but I know it's not good. Whenever I move, which is as little as possible, I can hear bones crunching and clicking. So I just lie here, and I watch the telly. The CCTV footage from London Zoo is pretty grainy, but that's Trev all right. You can tell in the way he moves, like a fucking bear or something, skirting the perimeter fence and looking for a way in.

I don't know how he got away from the police. The sound on the telly is all the way down, so I just have the pictures. I watch Trev as he shimmies under a hedgerow, emerging at the other side looking hunted and alert. I can't see his face, but I can tell he's fucking angry. There something about the shoulders – tense, and ready for a ruck. I've seen him looking like that before. Usually about five seconds before all hell breaks loose.

I feel a sort of churning in my stomach, and it's not from the drugs. I know Trev might have fucked me up royally this time, but you know, after everything, he's still a mate.

Suddenly, the camera cuts. Trev's being stretchered out of the zoo gates. In a body bag. I strain to hear the commentator, but the sound's low, and I have quite a lot of blood in my ears.

A zoo-keeper comes on – a fat bloke in a green uniform. I strain to hear what he's saying. I think I catch the words, 'local man ... night of drinking' and 'large mammal enclosure'. And then: 'the assailant was heard to call the hippo a –' they bleep it out, but looking at the bloke's lips, I'm pretty sure he said 'fucking cunt'.

They cut back to the gates. There are a few passers-by craning to have a butchers, but really no-one there seems to give too much of a toss. Trev's broken body is chucked in the back of an ambulance.

'The hippo,' concludes the reporter, in tons of solemn relief, 'was unharmed.'

And despite the pain, and the morphine sickness and the prospect of spending the rest of my life in a fucking wheelchair, I can't help smiling. Through everything, I find myself smiling.

And I think to myself: *I fucking knew it.*

O Happy Day …
David Bausor

'ELEVEN O'CLOCK IN PECKHAM RYE PARK:
COME AND CELEBRATE WILLIAM AND KATE'S
BIG DAY!'

'I don't know,' hesitated Mr Patel, looking at the flyer. 'There's bound to be trouble.'

'It will be a great day to be English,' said James. 'And there will be sausages.'

James had eaten many sausages in the past month. He still didn't know much about the English, but he knew that they sure loved sausages.

'Of course I'm proud to be English,' said Mr Patel. My ancestors fought with the Rani of Jhansi in the Indian Mutiny.'

Before he left Ohio, James had read all three volumes of Simon Schama's 'History of Britain'. Somehow, it was proving less helpful than he had anticipated. The problem was that everyone in this small island seemed to remember a different history than the one that he had read about.

'Hmm,' said James noncommittally. 'Wasn't the Rani rebelling against colonial rule? And didn't she lose?'

'Of course,' replied Mr Patel. 'What could be more English than to fight on the losing side?'

'I see,' said James, although he didn't.

The street party had been his father's idea. James Senior was a serious Anglophile who had never had a passport, but he was delighted when James had said that he was going to London. James himself hadn't been so sure. It was the first time that he had ever left America, and he found himself missing the familiar things. He called home every Sunday.

'A Royal Wedding! Street parties! Like when Princess Di married that guy with the ears,' enthused James Senior. 'You gotta go!'

'There don't seem to be any on around here. Maybe there'll be one in Trafalgar Square.'

'No, you gotta keep it local. You organise one for your street James, that's how.'

'I don't know,' said James. 'It seems kinda presumptuous.'

After all, he was only an exchange student. Two years into his degree at the University of Ohio, a year abroad studying Fine Art at Goldsmiths had seemed like a great escape. In his spare time, James painted landscapes, mostly pale blue skies over endless flat fields. Sometimes he painted in a tiny cow, but he never got the faces right. James loved Turner, but he couldn't paint like him. England was Turner's country: he felt like he owed the English. He made up some flyers and walked through Peckham, trying to hand them out.

On Lordship Lane, a skinhead struggling with a pitbull took a flyer. The skinhead had an upside-down Union Jack tattooed on his neck.

'I love them Royals!' said the skinhead. 'Salt of the earth. And sausages! Mugabe here loves sausages!'

'Sure,' said James, moving away quickly from the excited dog straining against its leash. 'Something for everyone.'

In Tescos, the cashier who scanned his Pot Noodles shook his head.

'This be some Babylon ting, man. Not for de brethren.'

James tried not to stare at the cashier's head, where ghostly pale scalp showed up between tight cornrows. His nametag read, 'Hi, I'm Sebastian Fortescue-Smythe!'

'Come if you can, Sebastian. How often does a prince get married?'

'You get another chance if this dude be anyting like his

Dadda,' replied Sebastian.

In college the next day, James waited until the end of the lecture.

'Erm.'

Most of the other students ignored him. In the front row, a girl with a large plastic bone through her nose was texting, stabbing the keys as if they were to blame for whatever had happened to her face.

James wasn't sure what to make of his fellow students. They didn't have people like this back in Ohio. The top students in his class were a Russian woman who electroplated dead cats into positions from the Kama Sutra, and an old Etonian who spraypainted 'This Wor(l)d Is Shit!' on billboards with human excrement. The students had clapped the cat bronzer, and they cheered the shit guy. When James had presented his own work – his best landscape, with two small cows – no-one had said a word.

'I have an announcement!'

Now they were all looking at him, even the girl with the nose-bone. He held up a flyer.

'It's a party because William and Kate getting married. Everybody's invited!'

No-one moved.

'Is it going to be, like, you know, an Event?' asked the shit guy. 'In the sense of an actual Happening?'

'Not really,' said James. 'But it's our chance to celebrate!'

Some muttering. A groan or two.

'There will be sausages!'

The students started to leave. James thrust a flyer at the nose-bone girl, holding it out until she took it. 'Please come! It'll be great!'

She has very blue eyes, he thought. Aquamarine, like a frozen ocean.

'Maybe.'

Then she was gone. He pasted the rest of the flyers up around the College.

Soon, he noticed graffiti starting to appear on his flyers:

'Kate is a slag.'

'Royal Family = Inbred scum!'

'William – call me b4 u do something crazy, we'll talk! Love always, Peter.'

He read all the graffiti carefully, but none of it seemed helpful. Mr Patel told James not to worry, and lent him a gas barbecue.

'You'll need a permit to use it in the park though.'

At the Town Hall, a clerk obscured behind a wire grille stamped the forms.

'Preparation of foodstuffs for human consumption, ten pounds. Permit for open fire, fifty pounds. And I'll need a credit card for the police bond.'

'What police bond? Why on earth would I need the police?'

'I don't make the rules, mate – the Prevention of Terrorism, Raves, and Other Anti-Social Behaviour Act 2010 does.'

James went to Tesco to buy sausages and buns. He asked Sebastian what the English drank.

'Pimms, of course. The taste of an English summer!'

James was already over budget, and he could only afford two bottles. He found plastic cups and plates. The plates had pictures of William and Kate. Their pink-cheeked faces were friendly but bovine. They didn't look like anyone he'd ever seen in London.

The day before the wedding, he rummaged through the pound shop. He bought twenty metres of bunting in red, white and blue. The only balloons they had left were bright green.

'Irish it up a bit,' said the assistant. 'It's only fair really.'

James bought a string of plastic Union Jacks to make up for it.

That night, he couldn't sleep. Early the next morning, he walked over to the park. The sky was grey and the grass was damp, but the day seemed full of possibilities. He lugged his kitchen table across the road and set up his portable radio. He brought all five chairs from his flat. If people wanted somewhere to sit, they'd just have to bring their own. James imagined his neighbours streaming out of their houses, bearing their chairs high while the aroma of grilling meat wafted all around. It took him hours to set up, stringing the bunting between the trees and blowing up the balloons. A couple of passing joggers looked curious, but didn't stop. He hummed as he worked, wishing that he knew the words to 'God Save The Queen' past the first line.

At ten o'clock, a police car pulled up and an enormous policeman got out.

'Good morning, sir. I'm DS Osundo.'

'Welcome to the celebrations!' said James.

'Not here to celebrate, unfortunately, sir. More of a watching brief for this demo of yours.'

'It's not a protest, officer,' James laughed. 'It's for the Royal Wedding! So we can all show how proud we are to be English!'

Osundo consulted a clipboard.

'Says demonstration down here, sir. How many are we expecting?'

James chuckled.

'You'll know that better than I will, officer. Fifty, a hundred? How many loyal English subjects do we have round here?'

'Hard to say,' said Osundo. 'You've got your Croatia versus Tunisia match on Sky this afternoon.'

The radio started to play wedding marches. In his heart, James knew that the nose-bone girl was sitting on a bus, getting closer. He turned up the radio and fired up the burners on the gas stove. Soon sausages sizzled and popped. Twenty buns lay split and buttered, with another twenty in reserve. He set out plastic cups and the two bottles of Pimms. The table looked a bit bare. Maybe people would bring their own salads and desserts, James thought. He should have put that on the flyer. He imagined sherry trifle, jam roly-poly – even spotted Dick, whatever that was. He looked around the small park. The trees were beginning to show spring leaves. Soon everybody would arrive. He hoped that he wouldn't run out of food.

At eleven o'clock, a young Vietnamese couple with a baby hurried by. They stopped momentarily, but then the baby started to cry. When James offered them a sausage, they examined it carefully and smiled before they shook their heads.

Soon afterwards, two men in dirty overcoats turned up. One wore a fur trapper's hat.

'Mmm, sausages,' said Fur Hat, helping himself. 'What's the occasion?'

'C'mon – it's the royal wedding!' said James. 'Haven't you heard?'

'Congratulationth,' said the other. His mouth was so full he was having difficulty speaking. 'Who'th the luckee lathie?'

'It's not me,' said James. 'It's William and Kate.'

'Cheers then, Bill,' said Fur Hat, drinking from one of the bottles of Pimms. 'But where's this Kate bird? Left you already?'

The other man laughed so hard that crumbs sprayed across the table. Then the pair went quiet, stuffing sausages into their mouths and passing the Pimms bottle back and forth. James hid the other bottle under his jacket.

'This is nice,' said James. 'But ...'

He was interrupted by a police siren. When the two men saw Osundo getting out of his car, they grabbed handfuls of sausages and ran across the park.

'Shiftless bastards,' said Osundo.

'They're my only guests,' said James glumly. He watched the two figures disappearing into the trees.

'Still bastards,' said Osundo, helping himself to a sausage.

It started to drizzle, and the wind grew gusty. Osundo

disconnected the gas burner.

'Health and safety,' said Osundo when James protested. 'You'd better turn that radio off.'

'Don't you want to know how the wedding is going?'

'Not really,' said Osundo. 'They're all much the same.'

'But this one is special!'

Osundo snorted. 'You sound like my wife.'

'Does she like weddings?'

'She likes them enough to leave me and marry someone else,' replied Osundo. He took another sausage and went back to his car.

James decided to leave the radio on and risk electrocution. People would want to hear the commentary, even if it was hard to hear over the sound of the wind. He waited for a while, but no one else appeared. James decided to persist a little longer – just in case the girl with the bone through her nose was late. The radio started to crackle.

'... an update on that wedding coming up – right after these messages!'

James ate a sausage while he listened to advertisements for Anchor butter and Toyota cars. The meat was lukewarm and greasy. He wondered whether he had cooked the sausages properly. Were they truly meant to taste like this? He thought he saw Mr Patel walking along the far edge of the park, but he couldn't be sure. The Union Jacks flapped in the wind, and he noticed that he had hung them upside down. When the radio dissolved into static, he turned it off.

It began to rain in earnest. A small lake formed on the grill, and the sausages started to float. James watched Osundo drive away. Perhaps William and Kate were already man and wife. He imagined the two of them on honeymoon, lying together in a hotel bed, as stiff and waxy as mannequins. In Ohio, the cows were waking up to another day of eating grass.

James felt like he didn't care if he never ate another sausage in his life.

But he packed the remaining food into a box and put it under the table. Then he climbed underneath the table too.

He couldn't imagine that Turner had ever had a day like this.

James decided to become a republican.

He took the Pimms from his jacket and drank, watching the bunting disintegrating under the force of the rain. Pimms tasted horrible, like peanut butter and jelly when you eat all the peanut butter first. He took another swig, and almost dropped the bottle when someone knocked on the table.

'Hello? Is it too late?'

James stuck his head out into the rain. It was the girl with the bone through her nose.

'I brought you something.'

She dropped a packet into his lap. He picked it up and read the label: 'Marks & Spencer Limited Edition William 'n' Kate Commemorative Sausages.'

'Thanks a lot,' said James. 'I think that I might finally get what the English are all about. Would you like to drink a toast?'

He held up the bottle and wished William and Kate all the happiness in the world.

Are We Nearly There Yet?
Emily Pedder

Before Christmas Mum took me up West. We went to Selfridges to try on the expensive perfumes, see if there were any freebies going. She walked around from counter to counter; I followed along behind.

'What do you think of that, Rae?' she asked, after she'd dabbed a bit on her wrist. I gave her my rating on a scale of one to ten, glad to be asked to help. We stopped by the Poison counter. Mum gasped. 'I love this stuff!' she squealed, running her hand down the purple curved glass.

She didn't buy any though. She said she'd told Mick she liked it and she hoped he'd buy her some. But she hung around the counter for ages, chatting to the assistants. They smiled and looked at me as if I was a cute animal. Mum patted my head, like she did when there were people to see her do it. After a while she said she had to go and do something and I was to wait for her by the Clarins counter. She said she'd only be a minute. I asked if I could go with her but she shook her head. 'Stay here,' she said. 'I'll be back before you know it.'

I stayed by the shiny counter and watched the beautiful ladies in their white coats and bright red lipstick, their hair carefully washed and combed, spraying perfume on passers-by.

The store was full of Christmas shoppers. People flooded in and out of the swinging doors. When I first came to London I used to think you could get stuck in those doors if you weren't careful; stuck forever, spinning around in glass segments.

One of the women behind the counter was looking at me. She was smiling and saying something to another assistant.

Now they were both looking at me, their mouths making 'O' shapes, as if they were looking at a baby. I turned away, towards the big department store clock that hung from the ceiling. Four thirty. I was sure Mum had been longer than a minute. I started wandering away from the Clarins counter and towards the other perfumes. When no one was looking I put a small bottle of Poison into my coat pocket.

Now I wanted Mum to be back quickly so we could leave, but I still didn't see her. I went back to the Clarins counter and walked past the different displays – the palettes of eye-shadows: pinks, purples, greens, just like Dad's paint box; the lipsticks jutting out like multi-coloured rockets. I ran my finger along the clear glass protecting all the boxes: moisturisers, face masks, body lotions, eye gels. A whole display of pretty white and red boxes with fancy writing, all made in Paris by the looks of things.

'Can I help you?'

It was the pretty woman who had been staring at me. She had blonde hair that folded in big shiny curls, and she was wearing misty pink lipstick.

'You look like you're after something?'

I dug my hand down into my pocket to make sure the bottle of Poison was still there. Did she know what I'd done?

'No, thanks,' I said, quickly, hoping to sound grown-up, like I knew what I was doing. Like I wasn't the kind of person who stole things. 'I'm waiting for someone.'

'I see,' she said. 'Well, while you're waiting, how about trying on some of our perfume?'

She smiled at me, a great big shiny smile, and now I could see her teeth: pearly white inside her misty pink mouth.

'Follow me,' she said, reaching out her hand and taking mine. I let her lead me. We held hands – she had soft, white hands – back over the fancy French boxes, along the eye-shadows, and the rockets of lipsticks, until we were in front of the perfumes. Then she let go.

'Roll up your sleeve,' she said.

I pushed my jacket up around my elbow, wishing my arms didn't look so scrawny.

'That's it,' she said. 'Now, what shall we try on today? Let's see. How about this one: a light and elegant scent with a touch of mystery. How does that sound?'

'Lovely,' I said. I was glad she had not noticed my arm. She had not noticed my arm and she thought I was the kind of person who would suit a light, elegant mysterious scent! I stood still as she held the bottle, cupping her perfectly manicured hands around the base and pressing the nozzle down with one short movement. A spray of bubbles covered my wrist. I waved my arm around, like I had seen Mum do, and then I smelled it. It smelt of flowers, pink honey-dipped flowers, the sort I used to smell sometimes on the way down to the beach, when we lived with Dad.

'It's beautiful,' I said.

'Well, I'm glad about that,' she said, and smiled again.

She was the fairy godmother in the Wizard of Oz. And I was Dorothy. I half expected her to disappear in a big pink bubble, or to wave her magic wand and whisk me and my red shoes away.

'I have to start packing up now,' she said.

'OK,' I said. Packing up? My heart started beating fast. Why would she be packing up? I looked at the clock. It was five minutes to five.

'What time do you close?' I asked, trying not to show my concern.

'Five o'clock, pet,' she said, but now she was busy and she wasn't smiling; she had things to do. The shop was starting to empty. A man's voice came over the loudspeaker; he said the store would close in five minutes. All the counters in this section were shutting down. It was getting much quieter in here, strangely quiet after all the noise and business and shopping.

Where was Mum?

My legs were tired. I slumped down onto the floor, my back against the counter. If I sat there she would find me when she came back from wherever she had gone. She would smell my flowery, elegant scent and then we would go home. Down there I could see people's feet as they left the shop: high heels, flats, boots, all moving towards the swinging doors that flipped them out into the cold. The floor looked less shiny from here. You could see the marks where people's shoes had been, each person leaving a trace of themselves along the shop floor, like thousands of snails. I concentrated on following each trail, as if they were lines on a map, working out how they intersected and over-lapped, where they began and ended. I built a whole network in my head. I worked as hard as I could at this so I didn't have to think about anything else. That was what I was doing when I heard her voice. She was shouting at someone.

'Take your hands off me,' she was saying. 'What do you think you're doing?'

Her voice was getting nearer. The store was getting quieter. I didn't look up. Maybe if I didn't say anything she'd stop. I kept following the trails: where did they end up, I wondered, whose house did they lead to?

'I'm not drunk. How dare you? Get your hands off me.'

I wondered what marks my shoes made. My red kickers had a chunky sole; they would leave a serious impression on the floor. I wondered if anyone would notice my tracks if I kept walking – kept walking and didn't look back.

'Rae. What you doing down there?' She was looking at me now. Her face was red and blotchy, her eyes glazed over. 'These people!' she was saying. 'I don't know what they want. I was just having a quiet drink and now they say I have to leave. What's going on?'

I stood up. She was looking at me but she couldn't really see me. Her eyes were as misty as the Fairy Godmother's lipstick.

There was a man in a white shirt and a navy jacket with gold buttons. He was wearing a peaked hat, ducked low on his head so you couldn't properly see his eyes. He put his arm around Mum, trying to hold her up, as if she'd fall down if he let go. The Fairy Godmother was looking at me again, staring and whispering to her friend as if she'd seen an animal run over in the middle of the road. I hated her now, hated myself for being tricked by her stupid girlie ways.

'Come on,' I said to Mum. 'Let's go.' I reached out my hand towards her.

'That's what I was trying to tell them,' she said. 'I just want to go home.'

The security man looked at me. 'I'll help you to the door,' he said. But I didn't want his help. I wished he would leave us alone. I wished he would bugger off and leave us alone. He started moving towards the exit, one arm around Mum who was dragging her heels. I was holding her other hand. We must have made a funny sight. Peaked hat was tutting under his breath, as if Mum was some kind of moron. I wanted to shout at him. I wanted to spit at him and tell him he was the moron with his stupid hat, and his stupid buttoned jacket. Mum started wailing.

'What have I done?' as if she'd lost something, left something behind. I squeezed her hand. Luckily there was a bus waiting outside the store and the man helped me get her on. I didn't say anything to him, just left him standing on the pavement as I shuffled Mum into an empty seat. Within seconds she was asleep.

But when it came to paying for our tickets, I realised I didn't have any money. I had to search Mum's pockets but my fingers were stuffed into my gloves and I couldn't move them around properly. The driver sat there, drumming his fingers on the wheel as if he didn't believe I was going to pay. Eventually I found her purse. There was just enough for the two of us to get home. The driver gave me the tickets and tutted as I walked away. People were staring at me. There was a girl about my age with her mother. They were surrounded by bags of expensive things, presents wrapped with ribbon, and coloured string. The girl was looking at me. 'Don't stare,' her mother said pulling the girl away but it didn't stop her. 'What are you looking at?' I said, scowling, as I sat down next to Mum. The girl turned quickly away, scared. I scowled again, just to be sure.

As the bus crawled along Oxford Street, I looked out of the window: street sellers with their fake perfume and roasted chestnuts; men in thick overcoats, steam from their mouths, as they hurried to find something for their wives; kids with mittens and red cheeks, staring at the toy displays. I thought about all the buses, weaving their way through the streets of London, red lozenges carrying people, zigzagging across the city. I wondered if Dad was sitting on one of these buses. I wondered what he was doing for Christmas. If he was even alive.

I patted my pocket to make sure the bottle of Poison was still there. Then I looked at Mum. Her eyes were starting to open. There was a spool of spit dribbling from her mouth. I wiped if off with the tip of my glove.

'Are we nearly there yet?' she said.

I nodded.

'Almost,' I told her, patting the top of her head. 'We're almost there.'

Rat
Liam Hogan

They say that in the City of London, you're never more than six feet from a rat.

Mine was called Boris.

When people said there was a rat following me, I didn't believe them. I assumed it was an elaborate joke, the sort of thing my brother would orchestrate. I'd laugh, and they'd shake their head and swear that they were sure they'd seen SOMETHING.

Then I saw the SOMETHING they'd seen running along a countertop. I only glimpsed it out of the corner of my eye, but it was fast, and brown.

I thought Mikey was taking things a bit too far this time. I mean a rat! In the kitchen? Tame or not, the things aren't sanitary. My landlord, if he found out, would flip. There was a strict 'No Pets!' policy; even goldfish were frowned upon.

But the sightings weren't restricted to my flat. I saw a dark cable-like tail disappear into one of the pigeon holes at work. Only, when I tentatively pulled out all of the letters for the NW6 postcode, there was nothing there. It was starting to get to me; I was beginning to see things.

And feel things. I was having a quick drink after work in the Posties – you might know it as the Kings Head, but no-one ever called it that – when something scurried over my shoe and brushed against my ankle. I must have jumped a mile, spilling my pint far and wide in the process. I nervously apologised and ducked outside for a calming fag. As I sat on the wall overlooking the trucks in the depot, I cursed my fragile nerves. A falling letter, someone stretching their legs out under the table, and my mind had done the rest. I was behaving like – well, like a kid being tormented by his older brother.

So when my holdall started moving in the changing room at the council gym, I wasn't scared. I worked it out. The locker was just large enough to hide in, if you were somewhat vertically challenged, and a length of cotton attached to the handles and gently pulled would make it twitch the way it was twitching now. But this time he'd been too clever – there was nowhere else to hide.

'Very funny. Come out Mikey, I know you're there.' I called.

And a large brown rat strode nonchalantly from between my bag and the locker. 'You got me,' it shrugged. 'But the name's Boris, not Mikey.'

I was gobsmacked. 'You – you've been following me around?'

'Sure.' He nodded. 'But I got tired of all the skulking. Decided to see what it would take for you to notice me. Quite a lot is the answer, you're really not very observant, are you? Though – officially – you're not actually supposed to see me. So do you mind if we keep this on the QT?'

And then he explained about the six feet rule.

'Wow. I thought that was just an average, just a statistic.' I mused.

'Yeah,' said Boris. 'A lot of people think that.'

I have to point out, because I haven't had a chance to do so until now, that this was no squeaky voice that Boris spoke in. If I had to imagine a rat talking – and for the benefit of those who are going to doubt my sanity, this is not something I regularly did – it would be a high pitched 'eee-eee' mouse sort of a voice, and not Boris's rather soothing baritone. I suppose this should have surprised me more, but I was far too busy being astonished that he was talking at all.

Which prompted my next question.

'Of course I can speak!' he chortled. 'I've been follow-ing you around for Thirty-eight years, and – and don't take this wrong – you're not exactly the strong silent type.'

I ignored the dig at my slight stature – it runs in the family – and latched onto the rest of his statement. 'Thirty-eight years? You've been following me since I was born?'

'Sure, like I said, one person, one rat.' He twiddled a whisker between his tiny fingers.

'But I thought that rats only lived for a couple of years. Five, at most?'

He rolled his eyes. 'I take it you read that somewhere. And obviously you value something written by some know-it-all human over a rat's personal experience. On the subject of rats. Sheesh.'

'Oh. I'm sorry.' I apologised, feeling somewhat lost.

'Well.' He huffed. 'You weren't to know. There are a lot of things you don't know.' He paused. 'Like what Mikey keeps in the third drawer of his dresser.'

'Excuse me?' I said, baffled.

'Suffice it to say, the next time your brother plays a prank on you, ask him how he's getting along with the deluxe model vacuum pump, and I guarantee that he'll leave you alone for a while.' He winked.

'Ermm, thanks.' I tried to dismiss the images that this conjured up. They weren't pretty. 'How the heck do you know about that?'

He shrugged. 'We rats talk. When you come close to another human, I come close to another rat. It's kind of a rat grapevine. We gossip, discuss the news, chew the fat – literally, in some cases. It's how we stay connected. Speaking of which, you should spend more time with Liz in Payroll.'

Again, I was baffled. I knew who he was talking about. Can't say I'd ever spoken more than a dozen words to her, though, because I also knew when someone was out of my league. 'Elisabeth Ramsden? Why?'

'Oh, her rat's a real honey. Lovely glossy coat. Must be

all of those Special K cereal bars.' He scratched behind his ears. 'Though... I suppose that doesn't really matter now.'

'Oh? Why's that?' I wondered how Liz would react if her rat started talking to her. If she was anything like most women I'd known, she'd be a gibbering wreck spread-eagled on the ceiling.

He stared at me hard. 'Look, you haven't asked me the most important question.'

Now, there were plenty of questions that I hadn't asked. Like how Boris could follow me on the Tube; or what happened when I went on holiday. But these didn't seem like particularly important questions. So I gave in and asked him which question he had in mind.

Boris sighed. 'Why do we follow you around?'

'Okay.' There was a long pause. 'So. Why do you follow us around?'

'I don't know.' He replied petulantly. 'I used to think it was so that we could keep tabs on you – find out where you were storing your food, or where you'd put down the poison, that sort of thing. But now – well I don't think they even bother to read my reports. So I have a new theory. I think they want us to stick close to you, simply because they want us close to you – as close as possible without being caught. Flea-hopping distance. How well do you know your history?'

'So-so' I admitted.

'Well, what about the botched attempt of 1665?' he asked.

'1665?' I scratched my head. 'Ermm. Well I know about 1666 – the Great Fire of London?'

'Which didn't help, but – come on man, what preceded that?'

I felt like I was back in school, with an exasperated teacher, and at that moment the penny dropped. Rats, plus the Great Fire of London. Equals –

'The Bubonic Plague?'

He nodded slowly. 'Close enough. Not actually Yersinia

pestis – that had been around for centuries – but easily mistaken for it, and unlike Yersinia, not fatal to rats. Well, the old grapevine has been buzzing lately. Nothing concrete, just snippets of internal news – odd requisition orders, promotions in the Lab Rat divisions, sightings of black rats at HQ. Put them all together, and I think we might be getting ready to try again.'

'Try again? Try what again?' I asked, befuddled.

'Wipe out the humans, of course. Anyway the point is, me and some of my mates, we're not exactly pleased with the idea. I mean, we do pretty well living under your feet, once we've learn to avoid the traps. Your homes are warm, not so well maintained that we can't get in, and the food! There's always something new to try if you don't mind wading through the garbage – and of course, we don't. But despite all of that, someone has been rattling our cage, and I keep getting the feeling that we're merely pawns in someone else's game. Well – no longer. We're deserting. We're going somewhere we can live free with no orders, no schemes, and no rat poison. Basically, a very long way from here.'

'How?' I wondered aloud. It was a lot to take in, and I wasn't doing a very good job of it, so you'll have to forgive me if my questions seem to indicate I was missing the big picture. Chances are – I was.

'There are tunnels.' He said darkly. 'Odd tunnels. All over London. Some of them pop up places you wouldn't expect, much further away than you've travelled underground. Some of them – go places.'

He stared at me. I stared back.

'What?' I'm afraid I still wasn't getting the hang of it.

'Ah, you wouldn't understand.' He waved his paw dismissively. 'Ground dwellers never do. Anyway. Now that you've spotted me, I shall bid you adieu. And some advice – watch out for the black rats, I'm sure they're behind this latest project, and rumour is, they're callous bastards, with a score to settle. Which does not bode well for mankind. Oh, and if anyone asks, you ain't seen me, right?'

Well, I guess you know the rest. The plague hit in the summer of the next year; the 100% mortality rate left millions upon millions of dead rats all over the city, though not one human fatality. Hardly even a sniffle. Seems Rat Flu was particularly specific – we were more at risk because of all the corpses rotting in the summer heat. The clean-up was massive. They called for volunteer squads, and I found myself working next to Liz Ramsden, collecting the decaying bodies and emptying them into the skips. Love blossoms in the most unlikely of places. Turns out she wasn't squeamish at all. Turns out she had a heart of gold and a stomach of steel, and a soft spot for short men. We're expecting our first child in the spring.

I do hope Boris made it out of the city, and I hope he took Liz's rat with him. If he did, then I guess it's an all's well that ends well sort of story. Except for one thing.

All the rats that we cleaned up were brown.

Not a single Rattus rattus – the black rat.

But rather a lot of them have been seen recently. The scientists say that they're opportunists, filling a niche, and filling it quickly. Up to six litters of ten rats a year. Well, you do the maths.

And I think back to Boris's warning.

I looked it up. On Wikipedia. The brown or Norwegian rat, Rattus norvegicus, wasn't native to this country, but once it invaded, it left little room for its competitor, the black rat, and the brown rat rapidly went on to become the second most successful mammal on the planet.

So, what if this wasn't another botched attempt? Maybe it went perfectly to plan, except we weren't the target, and it was the black rat who pulled the trigger? Revenge for nearly three hundred years of oppression?

Because that's the other thing I learnt. The clincher, if you will. Boris's ancestors didn't get to these shores until around

1728, more than fifty years after the Fire of London. Which means the Black Death could only have been spread by black rats.

I've stopped putting down rat poison, and convinced Liz not to get a cat. But still I worry. Because I now know the most important question that I should have asked Boris, and it isn't the one he thought it was. It's this:

Just how long does a rat hold a grudge for?

The Escape
Emily Cleaver

It's Lionel Levett who releases the bull, unhitching the hasp from the ring through its nose. He watches it slip between the wooden boards of the stall and into the street, smooth as a ship launching. As it sails past he reaches up to douse its wide, warm flank with a splash of lemonade from the glass bottle in his hand.

The bull reminds Lionel of his father, and if there's one thing in the world Lionel would like to do for his dad, it's set him loose. Nev Levett owns a market stall selling the scrap silver that stains his hands black with sulphide. Sometimes Lionel finds his dad stretched out under the stall with a handkerchief over his face like a corpse, but he isn't sleeping, he's shaking. Annie, Lionel's stepmother– that's who Lionel blames. Annie has a sting like a gadfly when she gets going. So the bull, sweltering in its stall in the Cally Market, makes Lionel think of his dad, and so off the chain comes and out the bull goes. Lionel watches after it with the feeling of a job well done.

Perhaps lying under things runs in the Levett family. Three streets away, Frank Levett, Lionel's older brother, is lying on his back under the kitchen table. He's naked. The reasons for this are complex and various. Frank has liked to lie on the floor since he was a child – his mother sometimes had trouble getting him to stand or walk at all. Frank preferred to wriggle on his stomach like a snake. Things, Frank has always thought, look different from the floor. It changes your perspective, makes the familiar strange and the small familiar. Plus, it's August, it's hot, and the dark cave formed by the checked tablecloth is a shelter from the sun that floods the room; and from other things too. Why is Frank naked? He has just nearly had sex with his step-mother

Annie. Just nearly, because Frank, standing in front of Annie's bed with his clothes already in a heap at his feet, suddenly scooped them up and ran from the room.

Annie hasn't bothered following him yet. In the meantime, under the table seems as good a place to consider the situation as any. Frank hasn't slept with Annie before, but he has had what he considers impure thoughts about her. He also has impure thoughts about Sarah Davey, whose dad runs the grocer's stall on Market Road. She has a well-developed chest for a fifteen year old, and wields it like her only weapon, standing with her hands on her hips and her legs apart like the Colussus of Rhodes. Recently he's been thinking impure thoughts about Annie and Sarah more than he's been thinking about cigarette cards, which is still mostly what he thinks about the rest of the time. He's one away from the full Tottenham Hotspur set, with only goalie George Clawley missing. Frank's dreams at night are an exciting muddle of Annie, Sarah and the elusive George.

Annie has had impure thoughts about Frank too, who's tall for sixteen, and already has the shadow of a moustache. You can't really blame Annie for this, in her opinion. She's only thirty herself, and her husband Nev is a useless lug with black hands and a red forehead, and all she's got out of life so far are two children that aren't her own and the run of two dingy rooms above the Cally Market that stink of cow shit on Mondays and Thursdays and rattle with the racket from the silver stalls on Tuesday and Fridays. She's entitled to a little enjoyment, she reckons. Not that she's getting up and chasing after Frank though. He'll come back soon enough, that's Annie's assessment of the situation.

So Annie lies and listens to the distant clatter and shout from outside, where the bull has reached the Market Road and is swinging down the middle of it through the crowd like a bowling ball through skittles. In the kitchen, Frank stares up at the underside of the table. It's made from the lid of a packing crate and the word SEVILLE is stamped across the underside of the boards in a murky red ink. Frank knew the shape of this mysterious word before he could read, tracing it like the map of a tortuous red road. Now he reads it with new eyes, and sees that there's a message in it, one that's been waiting here for him to discover all his life, hidden in plain sight. The hot red word, EVIL.

Frank crawls out from under the table and puts his clothes on. He shuts the door quietly behind him and creeps down the stairs and into the street. He can hear the market from the doorstep, the din of the crowd and the bellow of the animals, and it makes him think of hell.

Nev Levett is sitting in the Black Bull pub with his thick arms on the table, drinking porter from a pewter mug, sucking the froth from his moustache and thinking about dogs. Nev wishes he'd got a dog instead of another wife. A dog wouldn't hide his tobacco or tell him not to grind his teeth. But his wife won't hear of a dog. So Nev is picturing the dog he should have got, with a sagacious face and a glint in its eye, when the bull passes the window. It has just tossed over a haberdashery stall and caught a length of white taffeta on its horns, so it looks like a massive, stately bride coming down the street, with a train of boys, shop assistants and cattle drivers shouting and jostling along behind it. The bull is lost in the labyrinth of streets and pens, a hot maze at the centre of which the bull remembers its stall as a haven of cool shade. It is trying to get back there. Occasionally one or two of the braver men will make a dash for the ring through its nose and not quite reach it, ducking away from the sweep of its pitchfork horns as it turns.

The bull reminds Nev Levett of someone. He feels strangely sad, jealous almost, as if he is watching another man succeed where he has failed. He downs the porter and hurries from the pub, pulling his flat cap low over his brow and jingling the change in his pocket.

Lionel has a scientific mind. He likes to watch, to set an

experiment going and follow it to its conclusion in the spirit of rational enquiry. The results may prompt him to raise an eyebrow, or nod at the confirmation of a hypothesis. Lionel has been following the bull's path, from the stall where he set it going, to the point where it is now. Its trajectory is as interesting to him as the curve of a ball or the acceleration of a bullet to a physicist. So Lionel is in the crowd, swigging occasionally from his lemonade bottle, his cap pushed back on his forehead and his shirtsleeves rolled up in the heat. It gives him a bit of a turn to see his dad fall into step by his side, because Nev Levett and the bull have the same look of earnest confusion at the way things have turned out.

'Alright, dad. Bull's out.'

'Son. Seems that way.'

And now, Lionel is watching his dad with renewed interest, because there's something precarious in the old man's eyes, and Lionel's wondering what it will lead to.

Frank Levett is on Maiden Lane. The heat is opening him out like a peeled orange, tender and ripe and slightly swollen. Frank is preoccupied with the question of whether nearly sleeping with your stepmother is counted as incest. The warning message from the underside of the kitchen table is printed over everything, and when he blinks he sees Annie on the bed, breasts small as satsumas in Christmas stockings, belly button staring at him like an eye. His face is flushed, and he keeps the church steeple of St Mary Magdalene in sight like the peak of a mountain he's climbing. He draws level with Davey's stall, and there's Sarah, with her red mottled arms clutched together below her chest, the top tie of her dress undone.

'Hot, ain't it?' she says, and Frank throbs so dangerously all through his body that he runs past without saying a word.

On Market Road, Nev Levett has parted the crowd like a rock in a river and Lionel has followed in his wake. They're right up front near the bull. Then a window in the building above them crashes open and a woman screams. Whether she's screaming at the sight of the bull or at something more sinister inside the house is unclear, but the bull snorts and pirouettes on the spot as nimbly as a ballet dancer, so that it's facing the crowd. And at the head of the crowd are Lionel and his dad Nev.

The bull roars. The heat, the dazzling white of the material caught on its horns, the cobbles slippery with dung and cabbage leaves under its hooves and the roar of a passing train, all send him into a frenzy. It charges.

The crowd scatters, down side streets, into doorways, through windows, behind fences. Lionel and Nev dive under a barrow. They lie in the straw and muck, staring at the wooden boards above them.

And it's right at this moment, when the bull is spinning and roaring in crazy circles in the empty street, that Frank Levett turns the corner. Frank and the bull stop. There is something indefinable in both their eyes. In Frank's it could be something like the recognition of a deserved fate. In the bull's, it's more like a pleading for peace. They face each other.

Under the barrow, Nev Levett is hanging onto Lionel's collar.

'What about Frank, dad?'

Nev shuffles onto his side and looks him in the eye, then he's away, rolling out from under the barrow and springing to his feet, in between the bull and his oldest son.

In this moment, from under the barrow, Lionel suddenly sees the threads between everything; the ones that move us all around in the big, beautiful puppet theatre of the world. There must be threads, Lionel thinks. What else could explain the trajectories of father, brothers and bull, here, to this street, on this sunny afternoon? Lionel knows now that it wasn't him who set the bull going, even though his hand slipped the chain.

Nev Levett makes himself wide, flinging his arms open,

because someone in the pub once told him that's what you do with bears. There aren't any bears in Camden, but it might work just as well with a bull, he thinks. The bull stamps its foot and starts to run. They are twenty feet apart, ten, five, and Nev is looking straight into the bull's brown eyes, and there's recognition there, flashing between them like a spark down a wire. For a moment Nev sees the puppet threads too, dancing him and the bull together. The bull catches Nev on its horns, twists him up and throws him casually as a bag of straw. Then it paws the ground in a puzzled manner and trots away, back to its stall. You can set a creature free, but sometimes it prefers its trap.

Frank and Lionel Levett run forward to pat and shake their dad's broad chest. Nev is staring up into the sky. It's far too big and deep, as if he's looking into a bottomless pool. Vertigo grips him and he closes his eyes. That's better. Now he sees the planks of the bottom of his own market stall above him, each whorl and line known to him like a secret language, and he feels safer; not like he's falling at all.

Stained
Laura Martz

When a tall, drunk suit at the bar backed into Lindsey, sloshing about an ounce of merlot across her pale blue Thomas Pink shirt, it felt like the day was having its last, mean laugh.

'Damn it!' she snapped. He didn't even notice, just shouted something at the barman and sidled away through the crowd with his hands full of pints.

Lindsey looked down at the stain and jammed her lips together, refusing to start crying again.

Jack's voice was still echoing in her ears. It had been more than an hour now, maybe two. Two hours of stomping down endless stretches of pavement. When he'd ushered her into his office at the end of the day, his 'Sit down' had been pitched lower than usual so it wouldn't carry. That was how she'd known it was bad news.

'You're not fitting into the team, Lindsey. You haven't been able to deliver. And, I'm sorry to say it, but I'm afraid the clients have found you – abrasive. Maybe that style worked in New York, but it doesn't play in London.' Before she could argue, Jack had shaken his sleek head and continued: 'I'm sorry, but I'm not going to be able to renew your contract.' He'd flattened his hands on the immaculate glass desktop and parked his gaze somewhere over her right shoulder. The words had been reverberating ever since.

At the end of her walk, with her feet bleeding, she'd used her last tissue to scrub at the mascara she knew must be all over her face and pushed open the heavy wooden door of the nearest pub. The Glass Half Full, read the letters on the window.

Half full indeed. Lindsey daubed hopelessly at the stain in

the ladies' and took refuge on a battered sofa sitting neglected in the gloom at the back of the pub. Closing her eyes, she gulped wine and listened to Serge Gainsbourg crooning from a speaker. Lindsey had liked music in college, but then had come what they called real life, and the songs had seemed silly. Funny how a passion could elude you like that.

From the sofa she looked down the room at the tables in front. Groups of workmates roared; a couple on a date exchanged tentative smiles and touches. No one else was alone.

Serge Gainsbourg went silent, and the live twang of an acoustic guitar reverberated through the dry babble. Lindsey looked to her right, toward the sound. In the corner opposite her sofa was a tiny stage, and on it a young man bent his dark curls over his instrument.

He strummed once or twice and spoke into the mic. 'Hi. I'm Nick Time.' Or that was what it sounded like. A blue light on the ceiling flashed into her eyes and then fell softly across his face. The crowd quieted down.

Nick Time began to sing and play. His voice was gentle. Lindsey closed her eyes and let it wash over her. The love song was trite, strung together out of words like 'you' and 'happy' and 'ever'. But the melody soared and crept, and she let it carry her along.

When it ended, a few drinkers clapped; the rest kept bellowing as if no concert was taking place. Down the room, a glass smashed. The singer smiled and struck up another tune. Pulled along again, Lindsey listened, pushing thoughts away.

Sometime during her third large merlot, Nick Time was singing a lilting lullaby, and Lindsey, melted into the sofa with her eyes closed, felt almost happy. Music. It was a balm. A gift. How had she forgotten?

Come and get me, fates, she thought, merlot wafting through her head and redolent on her tongue. Then her glass was empty. She set it on the sofa. One more? Three large glasses was already a bottle. But what the hell.

The song ended with a jaunty strum. 'Thank you all very much,' Nick Time said, amid moderate applause mixed with chatter. Lindsey opened her eyes and looked over. He was glancing around the room, acknowledging his audience. 'That's all from me tonight. I've got CDs for sale. If you're interested, come and find me at the bar. Thanks again, and good night.' For long seconds, he beamed straight at her, with keen dark eyes. She smiled back through her haze.

After a minute or two, she stumbled up to find him.

'Excuse me – You said you had CDs?'

He was shorter than she'd realised, and balding, and not as young as she'd thought. Lines and the onset of jowls gave him away. But his smile was welcoming. It took her forever to find her wallet in her cavernous Ferragamo bag.

He handed her the CD with stubby working man's fingers. On its cover, *Nic Tynan* was superimposed over a picture of him resting his chin on his guitar.

'Thanks,' she said. 'Great.' She stuck it in her bag.

'Hope you enjoy it.' He turned away, toward someone shouting into his other ear. People pushed toward the bar on all sides.

Lindsey snuck another look. Nic Tynan's jeans bagged at the knees, as if he'd been gardening in them. Worse, his worn blue shirt was stained with sweat at the armpits. He was just an unkempt middle-aged man after all. She could see him at home after his gig, eating fish and chips with a tin of beer in front of the telly in some dumpy flat. He probably had some pathetic day job, like driving a taxi. Job: she pushed the thought away.

She swerved through the steaming crowd and out into the still, cool night. She would get some air, maybe a drink somewhere, and then a taxi. At home, the CD might keep her brain quiet until sleep drowned it.

Lindsey walked, listening to the tap of her own shoes,

tasting merlot. Nick Time's face and voice kept returning to her. The way he'd sung up there, alone, all innocence and faith.

It couldn't have been more than ten minutes before the sky unleashed an echoing crack. Rain began to patter on the tarmac. Lindsey walked past newsagents and takeaways, turning corners, staying near the lights. Drops wet her skin and crept through her hair.

She turned around to go back to the main road for a taxi and almost ran into a man leaving a shop. It was Nick Time – Nic Tynan – his blue shirt splotched with rain, his guitar case on his back, and a pack of cigarettes in his hand. He recognised her and favoured her again with that open, childlike grin.

'Oh,' she gasped, stumbling out of his way. 'Hi.' Recovering her balance, she nodded in his direction and scurried on around him.

But he was going the same way, and walked behind her in the quickening rain. 'Thanks for coming to the show.'

'No, thank you. You were really good.'

An unfamiliar feeling rushed in. Something about him walking home alone in his sagging jeans with his guitar on his back. They were both a mess now, in the rain.

'I'm just getting a taxi,' she said, glancing back. 'Come on, I'll give you a lift.'

'That's very kind. But my car's just up the road.'

Just then, her foot came down and failed to meet pavement. She pitched forward over the kerb and her hands ground into wet grit.

'Are you all right?' His warm, rough hands helped her up. She wanted to keep hold of them.

'I'm fine.' She let go and wiped the dirt on her best suit in her embarrassment. It was soaked through now, anyway, ruined.

'Can I buy you a drink?'

'Thanks.' His voice was gentle. 'I should be going.'

They looked at each other for a second.

'I really did like your music.'

The corners of his eyes crinkled as he smiled. But there was no invitation there.

'Well,' she said. 'Good night.'

She fled past the shops and around the nearest corner. Down in the distance she could see the main road. The air smelled of burst cloud and wet tarmac. Rain trickled down Lindsey's cheeks. She tried to see herself as he had: a smartly dressed younger woman, out of his league, with a thing for musicians. He would prefer deeper, more sincere connections. She hadn't made herself clear.

Near the end of the street where it met the main road, she passed a shop with antique mirrors in its windows. She stopped and saw herself. Her hair hung in wet ropes. Dissolved mascara blackened her swollen face, and wine stained her mouth. The forgotten blotch across her shirt had spread and gone bruise-blue.

She clawed at her hair and wiped her face on her shirt. At the corner, a taxi paused to let someone out. She ran toward it.

The driver looked her up and down.

'South Kensington, please.'

In the back, the cab smelled like feet.

'Can I ask you something? What do I look like to you?'

His eye met hers briefly in the mirror. Then he signalled and pulled out into the main road. 'I'll be honest, love, you're looking a bit rough.'

She put her hands up to her face. They were still gritty. 'I work in a bank. I make a lot of money.'

'Do you. Where to in South Ken?'

'You know what? Let me out. I need to get out.' She shoved money through the opening in the glass.

On the pavement, she stood under an awning by some vegetables out of the rain and took out her phone. The shopkeeper edged over, eyeing her.

Her mother's number in America went to voicemail. 'It's me,' she said. 'I'm coming home.'

She went inside the shop. The proprietor followed. She pointed. 'Bombay Sapphire. No, the big one.'

Outside, she unscrewed the cap and started walking.

How to Win at Scrabble and Life
Clare Sandling

This is how I ended up breaking up with Helen, even though I really liked her.

She told me at the time, what you have to understand about my family is, they're quite competitive.

I didn't know what she meant. I was like; I can handle dinner at your parents' house.

I reckoned I could charm the pants off her Mum, Dad and sister. I'd already done it to her, hadn't I? I don't want to be vain but I'm easy on the eyes, yeah? I'm smart, too; I only left school at sixteen because it bored me. Helen couldn't believe her luck when I asked her out. She tried to pretend she was cool but she practically bit my hand off. I'll tell you how it happened, because that's what led to what went wrong at her parents' house that night three months later.

I was working at Travis Perkins at that time, and I was dropping off some plywood in the design workshop at her sixth form college when I first saw her. I mean, I saw the back of her head, this long hair like Lyle's Golden Syrup, and I could see she was playing Scrabulous on the computer. I was like, working hard, are we? She minimised the window and turned round all angry but when she saw me looking at her with the old eyebrows raised she bit her tongue and giggled. I have that effect.

So I was like, let's see the Scrabble then, and she was like, I can't, I'm supposed to be doing my coursework, but I was like, go on, and so she put the window back up again and I had a look for like five seconds and then I was like, 'WAKE' with the W there. And I leaned over her and pointed to the square at the top of the word 'INNER'.

So she was like, wow, and she added up the points and it was nearly 40, what with the triple word score an' everything. So I was like, yeah you see I'm a WINNER and she laughed, and then I was like, so are you going to give me your number then or what? And she was all middle class like, no, you give me yours and maybe I'll call you, so I gave her my number but I didn't have to worry about whether she'd call or not, I knew she was mine already.

So that's how I ended up going to her old folk's house and it all going a bit Pete Tong. I rolled up to the five-bed detached on Lakeland Crescent in my sports Peugeot which I'd only just had the suspension lowered on, parked up behind the Jag, and went in all shaking the Dad's hand and kissing the Mum, and yes thanks I'd love an aperitif.

But it got off badly right after that, when her Dad starts telling me what Travis Perkins is getting wrong in its business strategy. I'm starting to argue back until I realise he's got me on the defensive, so then I'm like, change of tack, what line of work are you in then? And he says, stocks and shares, pulling on his braces. So then I'm like, so what's up and what's down, and he laughs and says, if you want to know that, read the FT.

By that point her Mum has got dinner ready and it's this gastro-pub stuff, she's piled it into a bloody tower on the plate. If anything she's worse than the Dad because she pretends she isn't being competitive, but she's all like, so does your mum like cooking, Dean? Like she's saying, because there's no way she's as good as me, is there?

As for the younger sister, she isn't quite so sharp as the others but she's learning. She's like; I made garlic prawns in home economics.

So any amount of smiling and flirting and cosying up isn't working with this lot. The more you try to look interested in what they're saying, the more they despise you for being inferior. I'm starting to get pissed off and I'm looking at Helen across the table, she mouths the word sorry.

Anyhow I'm thinking of a quick getaway after dinner but her Mum is all like, oh no dooo stay – we like having some new blood around to play games. I don't like the way she uses the word blood like that. The Dad is like, Trivial Pursuit, but the sister says, oh no, you always win at that, that's not fair, and Helen's like, Dean's really good at Scrabble (which she doesn't know because we've not actually got round to playing it since that first day, we've been too busy shagging, but she's right, I do kick ass at Scrabble). Scrabble's for four people, so somebody has to sit out, so in the end her Mum sits out and the rest of us set ourselves up around the table.

Second word in, her Dad gets a score of 131, 'EXAMINED' coming down from the centre top triple word score and joining up with 'RIND', that Helen had started with. After this her Dad is so up himself it's a joke, and what's worse, I can't even seem to get into double figures, let alone triple. Even though he's already won the game, he still has to take ten minutes each go to get the most out of his letters. The sister is pissing me off with her squawking, but she's got more points down than me and Helen has, too. The Mum is like hovering round looking at people's letters and saying, 'I can see a good one you could have', which is starting to make my knuckles itch.

I've only got crap letters, and I'm about to put down 'EARS' for about twelve points when her Dad says, all full of himself, Dean, looks like you're the loser in the game I'm afraid, so I shuck the letters around and I put down 'ARSE'. Helen and the sister giggles and the Dad frowns. Helen is like, it's in the dictionary.

So the game goes round and I am starting to enjoy myself when I see what I can do with the letters I've picked out this time. I'm humming and harring about whether to do it or not, but when her Dad gets his second seven-letter word and I see the look on his face, there's no way I'm holding it back. I stick an 'S' and an 'E' onto the word 'HIT: 'SHITE'. Helen starts to look a bit sick but I'm like, it's in the dictionary, and it is. 18 points to me. Her Dad's mouth goes into this kind of line, and the play goes round in silence. Next go, her Dad puts down 'CURB' and I realise what he's given me. I look at Helen and I can see she's begging me to stop what I'm doing and she's praying that I don't have anything in my letters that I can use. I think of that golden syrup hair and I'm about to play a five-pointer and leave honourably, but then the Dad says, I hope you're not going to be a bad loser, Dean. He is looking at me over his half-moon specs with this smirk on his face.

So I put down 'CUNT' and her Dad stands up and says, right that's quite enough from you, and then I stand up and I'm about twice as tall as him and I'm like, that's what you are Mr Fieldwright, a CUNT, and then he goes mental and he's like, get out of this house now, and I'm like, fine but remember, I know where you live.

And that was the end of that, and the start really of what got me where I am today. It was her refusing to see me, and then me getting up on their garage roof in the night to knock on her window, and the police being called and me getting a caution. Then it was me phoning the house just to shout 'CUNT' when her Dad picked the phone up. Still makes me laugh thinking about that. When they changed their phone number I went round with the spray can, then November 5th came round so I thought I might as well go round with the fireworks.

You've got to understand how it just made sense, move by move. True, I didn't mean to set their fucking hall carpet on fire and put her sister in hospital, and, true, I was starting to think it was getting a bit out of control, but I was winning and I was lovin' it. Deep down I reckon I knew I wasn't getting Helen back but I needed to see that For Sale sign go up, to know I'd really beaten that bastard.

But what I've realised, in the time I've had to think, in

here, is that I shouldn't have let myself get hooked up on that one bird, nice though she was. Not when I can have my pick. The looks of an angel and a mind like a harpoon. I'm a winner, baby. You wait until I get parole.

Girl with Palmettes
Martin Pengelly

In front of the painting at Tate Britain, Bateman realised that he and Melissa had now not been having an affair for six months. Before that, they had not been having an affair for about thirty years and, presumably, after this they would go on not having an affair for about another fifty. Then one of them would die and they could go on not having an affair forever.

The painting showed a girl wearing a purple hat with an orange band. Bateman didn't feel particularly abashed by her steady gaze: this evening at a private view was not the prelude to some illicit tryst. It might qualify, in itself, as a vaguely unsanctioned appointment. Similarly, going to see Jeanne Moreau in *Dangerous Liaisons* at the Renoir last week had not been either dangerous or, really, a liaison. It had been a trip to see a film with a friend. A friend he had slept with, granted. As in slept, comma, with. Or as in not slept, but spent a few hours awake with, staring at a grey ceiling after a brief bout of rather ungainly wrestling. Twice.

He looked at his catalogue – *Girl with Palmettes* by Malcolm Drummond. Circa 1914. The first night, back at his flat, they'd kissed. Drunk tea. Kissed a little more. He'd got her on to the bed when she had pulled away, looked down, given his erection a rueful tap and retreated to the corner to smoke. Getting her out of the corner had been like talking a jumper down from a roof. She had left. He had sprayed Mountain Breeze and Pledge to cover Gauloise.

With a little imagination, the *Girl with Palmettes* looked rather like Melissa. She seemed slim and tall, despite the half-length canvas. Long nose. Darker, though. Bateman looked round. He could see Melissa standing clear of a bobbing sea of grey heads; Botticelli's Venus on a Saga beach holiday. Other gallery-goers. Empty-nesters up from Metroland.

Once, at a Lucian Freud retrospective, a friend of his mother had told him that galleries were the best places to pick up girls. He didn't doubt it – Walt, a retired maths teacher from Hampstead, seemed to have had a pretty good time of it in the sixties. But Bateman did doubt his own choice of venues. Not being sure where White Cube even was, and having been frightened by students with pink hair the only time he went to the Whitechapel, he tended to stick to Tate Britain and the Royal Academy. Age not being the barrier it once had been, he might still have had his pick. But if twenty-two-year-olds in skinny jeans left him stumped and gawping, what chance had he here? This place was less hip than hip-replacement. Sometimes he found sixth-formers looking at St Ives stuff or a student or two in with the Euston Road School. Bad idea. He buried his nose in his Moleskine notebook and tried, with some success, to look academic.

Drummond's girl stood – or sat, more likely – in front of her palmettes, which were stencils on a café wall. After that first night he'd met Melissa at a café, though not like this one. In Soho, near Carnaby Street; the kind of place where you paid £7 a shot for coffee made from beans pre-shat by Madagascan lemurs. They had talked about how they weren't going to have an affair, about how, technically, even if they had had one, it still wouldn't have counted as an affair. He had no one to deceive – except himself, of course – and though she did have a boy-friend he worked in the City and, apparently, had affairs of his own. The metaphysics of it all were too tricky for Bateman to really understand but, put as simply as possible, it couldn't have been an affair – had they had it, which they hadn't – if one side wasn't attached elsewhere and the other was but seemed to operate in some form of open relationship. That wasn't to say they couldn't have had something, but they hadn't. Bateman felt a little defeated. And light-headed.

He didn't know much about Drummond, other than that he'd taught art before dying in the forties, his chances missed and his name unmade. His mates, the Camden Town lot, Bateman knew all about. He'd done a Masters, during which, in his spare time, he'd written essays for a dark-eyed Rebecca who turned out to be attached to a floppy-haired Rupert. When their paths parted – Bateman towards modernists and trenches, she to a term's worth of polemics and crotch-shots in post-feminist photography – she dumped him for a single mother who had access to the appropriate books. The dark-eyed Rebecca now worked at a gallery near Berkeley Square; he was still stuck at the paper.

Drummond's girl had dark eyes and a light-blue streak up the bridge of her nose. The right side of her face was in shadow. After the Soho café Bateman had met Melissa in Borough, in a bar where old films were projected on to the walls. Hopped up on Bogart and Argentinian lager, he had mentioned their non-affair. Melissa, fermented by cocktails, had agreed to give it another go. In the cab, crossing Blackfriars Bridge, Bateman had felt a kind of exhilaration – one part impending sex to six parts simply feeling alive. Unfortunately, once in bed, guilt, rather than the appropriate part of his anatomy, had chosen to raise its head. Again, Melissa had retreated to the corner. Again, he had fetched Pledge and Mountain Breeze.

The girl's neck, framed by the white collar of her dark-blue dress, was picked out in oranges, greens and pinks. A meek post-Post-Impressionist touch, Drummond's belated response to Gauguin, Van Gogh and Co., abandoning Camden Town bedsits way too late in favour of fauve colours in a beastly coffee house off Fitzroy Square. Bateman could have made a point like that to pick up a mark in an essay or even, had he had the guts, to follow Walt's advice and try to pick up a mark in here. He'd taken a string of first dates to galleries, at least, but he'd cut his losses with Sandrine, a Frenchwoman introduced to him by the dark-eyed Rebecca. She'd turned at the end of an arduous hike around a Sickert show and told him she felt like a character out of Beckett.

'I can't go on,' she'd said. 'I'll go on.'

He looked round; Melissa must have gone into the next gallery. After their second night together – their affair clinging to life like a parched pot plant in a south-facing window – complication had arisen in the form of an orthodontist he'd met in a pub. Bateman, conscience aflame, made a pillock of himself at the Pillars of Hercules, trying to explain to Melissa why he was going to give things a try with the orthodontist. When the orthodontist, who'd been seeing someone else, dumped him for a third time – after he'd told her about Melissa – he appreciated that he might have made a mistake.

He still, however, saw Melissa. They watched a verse drama about Jack the Ripper in Dalston, physical theatre in Swiss Cottage and an all-male production of *The Women of Troy* under a bridge in Southwark. They listened to short stories in Fitzrovia, watched middling operettas at the Barbican and endured long nights of Nicaraguan socialist agitprop at the ICA. All things considered, their non-affair was proving pretty enduring. Perhaps one day they would run out of things not to talk about and, presumably, thus have to not get married in order not to restart the conversation they weren't having. Then they could not talk about the children they didn't have, not bore neighbours over dinner they didn't cook with chat about flats they weren't going to buy, and not end up in listless adulteries with the same neighbours that, it followed, they thus wouldn't have anyway.

Bateman looked at the label next to the painting.

'The woman's purple hat with orange band is reminiscent of the respectable but unremarkable clothing adopted by certain groups who prioritised practical dress over ornamentation, for example working women, those engaged in charity or social work, or demonstrators for women's suffrage.'

Pondering an idea for a Turner Prize-winning installation – a gigantic gallery label made of thousands of little gallery labels, full of nouns and syllables and signifying nothing – he found Melissa. She had skipped past listless nudes, slab-faced landladies and a few oils of horse sales and was sitting on a banquette in the last gallery. Projected on to the opposite wall, in the manner of *The Big Sleep* and *Key Largo* in that bar in Borough, were scenes from early twentieth century London. The reel lasted about five minutes. Bateman leant against the frame of the door. Most people stayed for a couple of turns, paying more attention to moving pictures than they had to the still ones before.

On the wall, after a football match and soldiers drilling, Emily Davison rushed out of the crowd at Epsom, to be knocked down by the King's horse. Under the jerks and scratches that made the preceding scenes seem comic, full of beetling old ladies and stop-motion policemen, here was simple, dreadful impact. Concussion; whiplash; fracture. Bateman winced. Perhaps a glitch in the old stock made the fatal moment worse, the jerk in Davison's falling body more unnatural, more sharp, than it must even have been. Life underlined by death. A gallows drop.

Outside, he bought a couple of glasses of soupy red and sat with Melissa at a rickety metal table, next to a beaky man in a cravat and his paisley-clad ruminant of a wife. Melissa talked about the exhibition, of a film at the Phoenix next week. She did not talk about their non-affair.

Sometimes he missed her. He had been away, to Edinburgh for the film festival, and as the train passed York and Durham he had thought fondly of that fond, thoughtful tap.

'Ah, well,' it had seemed to say. 'Some other time.'

It was the one moment of artless, honest intimacy they had shared. The one such moment he had shared with anyone for about five years, if he didn't count the woman who was sick on him on the tube.

Melissa could see through him. That irritated him a little, but then so could he, and women who didn't try to exasperated him beyond measure. The dark-eyed Rebecca and Sandrine had had his number from the start. He had built up an image of the latter as a kind of plaster-of-Paris saint, a Left Bank intellectual with great legs and a moue.

With Melissa, the attraction was professional, in a way. He was an editor but she was a good one. And she was editing him.

They finished their drinks and Melissa walked outside for a cigarette. Bateman had no idea whether she would stay with her boyfriend or not. Marry him or marry someone else. Marry no-one. It didn't matter, because he had – as with Sandrine, as with the orthodontist – missed his chance.

He bought a postcard of *Girl with Palmettes*. Melissa did not bring up the subject of their non-affair on the walk to Pimlico, or on the tube, or when they parted at Victoria. They arranged a trip to the cinema. *The Sorrow and the Pity* on Shaftesbury Avenue.

When Bateman got home, he propped the postcard on top of the novels on the shelf above his fireplace. He looked at Drummond's picture, then at the next postcard along. *Mr Wyndham Lewis as a Tyro*. From a show at the National Portrait Gallery. A satyr's grin. Piggy eyes over a billhook mouth. A puckish Priapus or – dear Masters markers of long ago – a priapic Puck.

'You have to laugh,' Mr Wyndham Lewis seemed to say, with a kind of malevolent insincerity. 'Don't you, squire?'

Bateman smiled back and, slowly, turned *Girl with Palmettes* to the wall.

Renewal
Joan Taylor-Rowan

'You could do some management training,' my boss says handing me my contract for renewal. We are expanding and there are opportunities opening up in testing the machines that test the smartcards,'

'…that live in the house that Jack built,' I say.

He smiles slightly, and tilts back in his chair, shuffling bits of paper in his hands.

'Anyway Rachel, think about it. You'll need to sign the contract and bring it in with you tomorrow. You have a future here with us. I know it's not glamorous but we don't work you too hard do we, so you've got time to dabble…'

'Yes,' I say, 'I like to dabble, I'm a real dabbler.' I can feel myself being too snide and my boss is not a nasty man. I leave the office clutching the contract, the weight of the decision pressing on my shoulders.

I am thirty years old, which as my mother says means I'm in my prime. Somehow she makes that sound like an accusation. I should be prime minister or on prime-time TV. She wanted me to work in an office when I was pretending to be a poet. But now I am working in one, she still isn't happy. She doesn't know how to describe what I do. If only I were a lawyer or a doctor – a one-word job with its own mini-series. At least I have a boyfriend. Don is a builder, it's a bit manual for mum's taste but he has ambition. Don is short for Don Quixote – his mum was reading it when he was in the womb. 'I wanted a boy with dreams,' she confided, one Sunday over lunch, as Don and her husband compared the IKEA and Argos catalogues for storage solutions.

'She has pretensions like you,' my mother whispered.

Normally I go to lunch with Sarah, but she's not in – her little boy is sick. She has two kids, both round and soft, who call me Auntie Rachel, it twists my heart when they say it. I think about having kids sometimes. Don says the pram in the hall is the death of creativity. Of course he didn't say it first but he thinks that knowing it is just as good. When I look at those two boys I think they are better than any poem bloody Larkin ever wrote. Is Don the death of my creativity? He wanted the big fat mortgage – its zeros, two eyes watching what I spend every month, staring at me as I think about giving up work to write full-time.

'I think it's just a hobby,' my mother says, though no-one asked her. 'If you were a real writer, you would be up before work scribbling away like that Danielle Steele. You just like the idea of being a writer.' She drops this bomb on me from time to time and it always goes off. A real writer. How do I get real?

The contract sits in my bag, a piece of plutonium with the potential to destroy stealthily. I open the folder called unfinished works – my dabblings. Each one I read fills me with mortification. Who do I think I am? I'm Unreal.

I take the contract out and sign it. 'Doing what you have to do, not what you want to do. That's what it is to be a grown-up.' I hear my mum's voice again, a conversation over dinner, where she likes to share the indigestible facts of existence.

I can't help wondering if disillusion is the D in my DNA.

I phone Sarah. Her boy is still sick, I hear him wailing in the background.

'I'm renewing my contract,' I say.

'What about despair, despondency and thwarted literary ambition,' she says referring to my morning email – and by the way you spelt thwarted wrong.' Stung, I hang up on her.

To cheer myself up, I leave early and stop for sushi to take home. Raw fish – risky my mum would say anxiously. But Sushi makes me feel adventurous. It's not an easy food. You eat it with sticks and a condiment that makes your eyes water and your nose run at the same time – it's a food that fights back.

The station is beginning to get busy, people hurrying in, heading for trains that might still have seats. In the middle of the concourse a man is lying on the floor. I noticed him out of the corner of my eye when I came in, a slip I assume or a fainting attack. He is still there a couple of minutes later as I leave the newsagents with my milk. A member of the staff is kneeling next to him. Other passengers like me turn their heads in his direction as they walk by, comforted by the sight of the female employee in the high-viz jacket.

The woman looks nervous. She is glancing around as if she's expecting someone to come. The man has not moved. People entering the station give him a wide berth. The announcer mentions two delayed trains but doesn't ask if there is a doctor on the station. They must know the ambulance is close. I can see the man more clearly now. He is young, bearded, probably the same age as me. I walk back towards him. She is trying resuscitation on him now but doesn't look as if she knows what she is doing. She is speaking into her walkie-talkie. She hooks onto my glance, desperation in her eyes.

'Is someone on their way?' I say. She nods rapidly. 'But it's rush hour, they're stuck in traffic, they've sent a motorbike paramedic, but he's been involved in an incident with a cyclist, so they've called for another.'

The man's skin is darkening to a bruised purple. I stare at his face.

'I think I know this man.'

'Do you', she says eagerly 'is there anyone you could phone?'

I shrug now, awkward, blushing. 'I mean I don't know him, he works in my building. He works on my floor. I think his name is Paul,' or is it Peter? I realise I know nothing about him. I try to picture any photos on his desk but I can't. I am unable to do anything. I have no useful skills. I cannot do First Aid and poetry cannot help me.

The woman on the floor is speaking into her radio again her voice urgent and hushed. She is resting her hand tentatively on the man's chest. I know instinctively that she cannot feel anything beneath her hand and that is why it is there so lightly. She does not want to feel the solid evidence of death. As I turn away I hear the booming request for a medic and I hurry on refusing to look back.

At home there is a message on the table from Don. He has tried to text me but my phone is off. He has gone to the pub with his mates and I can join them later if I want. He has drawn a heart at the bottom. It makes me want to cry.

I cannot eat. I watch TV but my mind can't engage with it. I pour myself a stiff drink. A stiff. I try not to think of that face. At nine I phone the transport police. After several attempts I get through to a woman.

'There was a man at Cannon Street station this evening', I say, and my throat is tight. 'He was unconscious and the ambulance couldn't get through the traffic, I think a medic might have helped him. I just wanted to know how he is.' Present tense.

There is a pause at the other end, some rustlings. The news is on the television, but there is no picture of his face.

A few moments later I hear her clearing her throat, 'Hello, are you still there?' She pauses, 'I'm afraid ... he didn't make it love.'

I let out a little cry, and bite hard on my finger.

'I'm so sorry pet, was he a friend?'

'No, not really, not at all. But he was there on his own. No one who loved him was there.' I am crying now, and feel like a fraud but I can't stop myself. 'The traffic ... the ambulance couldn't save him. He was young. I've been thinking about him all evening.'

'Oh, that's kind of you,'

I'm not kind at all, I want to say. I should have known more about him, I should have known his name.

'I'm sorry, you must think I'm really stupid but I kept thinking of his life over just like that, all his hopes and dreams gone!' I pause and blow my nose. The woman on the phone sighs. We are together for a moment in the silence. I don't believe in God but still I think of his soul floating around in the ticket office like a pigeon trying to find a way out.

'Are you going to be alright?'

'Yes, yes of course, it's just the shock?'

'I'm sorry love.'

I stare out of the window. It is dark, but the streetlights make everything glow. A couple walk by arm in arm, laughing. A man stops to adjust his iPod. Someone, somewhere, is staring at a phone that has just told them that their son is dead. I rummage in my bag for mine, and spot the contract. My heart beats rapidly like a moth against the window. I take out the stapled sheets and tear them into pieces. I watch them fall to the floor as white and redundant as the dead man's shirt. And then I ring Don.

I can tell when he answers that he is already a little drunk.

'Hi babe' he says, 'come on down. It's the pub quiz, we need you. We can't do any of the fuckin' poetry questions.'

I laugh a little. 'Will you be home soon?'

'Soooon' he says. 'As the moon...' I nestle the phone against my ear, and my eyes well up. I feel very tired. I want him here with me, the solid aliveness of him, his hot breath, his beating heart.

'Soooon as a spoooon,' he sings, 'As a spoooon in Junnne.' I can hear his mates snorting and I laugh despite myself, a tearful, gulping laugh. Oxygen fills my lungs.

'Stop that', I say 'I'm the poet remember?'

About the Authors

David Bausor is a south Londoner who has an MA in Creative Writing from Royal Holloway. He is working on a novel about a war crimes trial called *Ghosts in the Palace*. He has stories featured at Tales of the Decongested, and Bedford Square 4.

Emily Cleaver's short stories have been performed to audiences at Liars' League, WritLOUD, Tales of the Decongested and Spark London, broadcast on Resonance FM and Pagan Radio, and published in .Cent, The Mechanics' Institute Review, One Eye Grey and Smoke magazines. She also blogs on books for Litro Magazine. She lives in Oxford where she is involved in setting up the Oxford branch of Liars' League.

Katy Darby co-runs Liars' League (www.liarsleague.com) and teaches Short Story Writing and Novel Writing at City University, London. Her first novel, T*he Whores' Asylum,* was published by Penguin in February 2012 and will appear in paperback as *The Unpierced Heart* in September. Her personal website is www.katydarby.com. Katy is the co-editor, with Cherry Potts, of the Arachne Press anthology *London Lies.*

Simon Hodgson is a writer, editor and dad based in San Francisco.

Liam Hogan has been writing short stories for Liars' League every month for more than 4 years, occasionally they select one to keep him sweet. He also submits to Liars' League Leeds, and is hoping for a hat-trick with Liars' League NYC. Shorts have also appeared in *Litro* and been read at StoryTails, and at The Post-Apocalyptic Book Club. A novel is mooted, though it is only currently the same length as his shorts. He lives in London.

Jason Jackson started writing again in April 2012 after a long hiatus. He hopes to build on the extremely limited success he had the first time around. He keeps a writing progress blog at tryingtofindthewords.blogspot.co.uk

Laura Martz is a long-term expatriate American writing about cultural dislocation. A former journalist, she has published numerous stories and articles in print and online publications including Litro. She is going to get an agent for her novel this year if it kills her.

Alan McCormick is a regular contributor to the Liars' League and his stories have appeared in many places, including the Sunday Express, Matter, Aesthetica and Litro.
'DOGSBODIES and SCUMSTERS', a collection of Alan McCormick's stories and Jonny Voss's illustrations, is available from www.roastbooks.org. See more of Alan's stories and his illustrated writing at www.scumsters.co.uk and www.3ammagazine.com

David Mildon is an actor and a playwright, who pays the gas bill by telling tourists the story of London. However, the woman he loves prefers listening to tall tales, so sometimes he writes them down.

Emily Pedder is an award-winning writer based in London. Her short stories have been published in several magazines, including Mslexia and Thirteen Stories. She is the recipient of a Commonwealth Short Story Prize and an Arts Council Award. She currently heads up the short writing courses at City University.

Martin Pengelly is a freelance editor and writer who edits and writes for *The Guardian*, *The Independent* and *The Times*. He is an editor and writer for The Fitzrovia Radio Hour.

Cherry Potts is a Londoner. She is author of two collections of short stories: *Mosaic of Air*, and *Tales Told Before Cockcrow*; a diary of a community opera *The Blackheath Onegin*, and has several stories in anthologies. She is has completed a Lesbian Fantasy Epic, and is currently working on her next collection, a science fiction novel, and a timeslip-young-adult kinda thing. She runs workshops for writers exploring NLP (Neurolinguistic programming) approaches to language and characterisation; and is the owner of Arachne Press, co-editor of *London Lies* and editor of *Stations*.

Clare Sandling's stories have been performed at the Liar's League and Tales of the Decongested. She has completed a novel, *The Residence of Queens* set in a claustrophobic care home, and is now working on a children's book. She is a member of the Willesden Green Writers' Group and Brockley Writers Of Our Age.

James Smyth was born in a small town in West Yorkshire, and moved to London to seek fame and fortune as a writer. The fortune hasn't arrived at the time of writing, but the fame must surely be just around the corner.

Rosalind Stopps lives and works in South East London, which provides endless inspiration. She has an MA in Creative Writing from Lancaster University and is currently working on her third novel.

Joan Taylor-Rowan is a teacher of Art and Textiles, and world traveller. She is the author of *The Birdskin Shoes*, a tale of circuses and earthquakes in Mexico. She has had several stories read on Radio 4 and performed at Short Fuse, Storytales, Liars' League and Tales of the Decongested. She is currently writing a musical with a composer she met through Liars' League.

Harry Whitehead is an author and academic who teaches creative writing at the University of Leicester. he worked for fifteen years in the film business before becoming a professional writer. His novel, *The Cannibal Spirit*, is published by Penguin Canada, and has been described as 'powerful, brave, ambitious,' (The Globe and Mail), 'a thriller with a Joseph Conradian plot' (The Walrus), 'a unique work, compelling, complex, thought-provoking and impressive' (Quill and Quire). He has published short- and non-fiction in a variety of genres.

Laura Williams is a novelist in search of an agent and/or publisher. She has had a few stories published in anthologies and online including *Back Fat* in Tales of the Decongested Volume Two and *Balcony View* in Mechanics Institute Review Volume Four. She received a distinction in the Birkbeck Creative Writing Certificate. She'd like to believe that the pushchair in the hall won't stop her from putting fingers to keyboard again sometime soon. Laura lives in Harlesden with her husband and son.

To everyone's great relief, Nichol Wilmor did not follow in his parents' footsteps and join the theatrical profession. Instead he became a random traveller, an unreliable teacher and an accidental publisher. He now lives in London where he writes – very slowly – under different names.

About Arachne Press

Arachne Press is primarily a publisher of fiction, particularly short fiction. We aim to showcase new and established writers in a series of collaborations with Liars' League and in other unconnected anthologies and collections. We will also publish poetry, novels, fiction for children and selected non-fiction.

London Lies is our first book, and our first Liars' League showcase.

Our next book, *Stations*, is a collection of disparate stories that are connected by the Overground line in East and South London.

From tigers in a South London suburb to retired Victorian police inspectors investigating a series of train based thefts, from collectors of poets at Shadwell to life-changing decisions in Canonbury, by way of an art installation that defies the boundaries of a gallery, *Stations* takes a sideways look through the steamed up windows of the Overground train, at life as it is lived beside the rails.

A story for every station from New Cross, Crystal Palace, and West Croydon at the Southern extremes of the line, all the way to Highbury & Islington.

Information For Writers

Arachne Press will start considering unsolicited submissions in April 2013.
In the meantime we are running occasional workshops for writers led by Cherry Potts. You can find information about these on our website.

About Liars' League

Since 2007, Liars' League has been the place where professional actors read brand-new short stories by rising (and sometimes established) writers. Every event is themed, and submission is open to any unpublished story (subject to length) from any writer, anywhere in the world. Liars' League takes place on the second Tuesday of every month at the Phoenix Pub, Cavendish Square, London (near Oxford Circus tube) and if you would like to join us or find out more:

Our website is www.liarsleague.com.

You can email us on liars@liarsleague.com, follow us on Twitter @liarsleague – or just come along.

Writers write. Actors read. Audience listens. Everybody wins.